CAMERON DOKEY
KATHRYN JENSEN
JEAN THESMAN
SHARON DENNIS WYETH

AVON BOOKS PRESENTS

Be Mine

It's February—a time to warm your heart with stories of love and romance from four of your favorite writers. *Cameron Dokey, Kathryn Jensen, Jean Thesman,* and *Sharon Dennis Wyeth* bring you all the excitement and suspense of dream dates, valentine cards, the agonies of a long-distance romance, and a modern-day Romeo and Juliet love story. It's the month for dreams to come true, so settle back and read about those magical moments that may soon be yours . . .

Other Flare Romance Anthologies
from Avon Books

NEW YEAR, NEW LOVE
A NIGHT TO REMEMBER
SEE YOU IN SEPTEMBER

Be Mine

CAMERON DOKEY
KATHRYN JENSEN
JEAN THESMAN
SHARON DENNIS WYETH

AN AVON FLARE BOOK

BE MINE is an original publication of Avon Books. This work, as well as each individual story, has never before appeared in print. This work is a collection of fiction. Any similarity to actual persons or events is purely coincidental.

AVON BOOKS
A division of
The Hearst Corporation
1350 Avenue of the Americas
New York, New York 10019

Published by arrangement with the authors
Library of Congress Catalog Card Number: 96-96912
ISBN: 0-380-78704-0
RL: 6.7

First Avon Flare Printing: February 1997

Printed in the U.S.A.

RA 10 9 8 7 6 5 4 3 2 1

Contents

Talking Tradition

Jean Thesman

"I wish my parents didn't make me go to your house after school," Will Storey told Laurie Miles. He kicked a lump of slush off the sidewalk to emphasize his remarks.

Laurie glanced sideways at her twelve-year-old neighbor, whose head was buried to his red nose in a big plaid scarf and knit cap. "Stop complaining," she said. "It's only for a couple of weeks. And I wish *you'd* stop telling people that I need you to help me after school with my homework." She kicked a lump of slush, too.

She hadn't paid much attention to what she'd been saying to him, because she was watching a tall, blond boy walking alone, half a block ahead. It was hard to concentrate on anything but Kai Jensen when he was in sight.

Will, whose wire-rimmed glasses had slid to the end of his nose, glared at her. "You're mad because I'm in advanced placement, and I'm a senior and you're a freshman."

"But *I'm* not *weird,"* Laurie declared automatically. They'd had the argument before, a zillion times. It was almost a walking-home ceremony.

The blond boy was pulling away from them. Laurie walked faster so she could keep him in sight. He was more than six feet tall. His hair was blond, almost silvery, and his eyes were the exact color of her Siamese cat's.

Will didn't snap back at her the way she expected.

He was silent while they passed snow-covered yards and dismal piles of dirty slush heaped beside driveways and walks.

Finally Laurie glanced over at Will and saw him marching along, head down, blinking furiously.

"Sorry," she said. "You aren't weird. You aren't even the only twelve-year-old in advanced placement. But here I am, just a freshman, and I'll be fifteen next summer. And you're all anybody in the neighborhood ever talks about."

"Oh lucky me," Will said sourly.

"And," Laurie went on, "I think your parents should let you use the computer as much as you want, instead of sending you to our house to watch Mom do watercolors of birds."

"I'm *never* going to be an artist," Will griped. "Everybody knows that except my parents."

"They want you to try everything," Laurie said. "And Mom volunteered . . ." She stopped talking. The tall boy had turned a corner ahead, but he had glanced back first. Had he seen her? The idea struck her speechless.

"Aw, jeez," Will complained. "You're leering at Kai Jensen again."

"I'm not leering!" Laurie said.

"Ogling, then," Will said. "You'll scare him so much that he'll move back to Denmark."

"Be quiet or I'll tell everybody you've got a crush on Vanessa King, and she's older than you and lots taller."

"Less than an inch," Will said. His face was red. "And she's only a year older."

"She's a freshman," Laurie said. Kai was out of sight, and the February day seemed even drearier.

"What would you two talk about? She doesn't know any more than I do, and you're always telling me I'm boring."

Will wasn't listening. "She collects fossils. I told her about mine and she said she'd like to see them."

"Oh, wonderful. Come up to my room and look at my million-year-old toenails," Laurie muttered.

"What?" Will asked. "What are you mumbling about?"

"Nothing," Laurie said. They were nearly home, and she had to cheer Will up. Her mother didn't like it when they argued. "Are you going to the Valentine's Day mixer?"

Will stared at her. "Are you crazy? Why would I do something like that?"

"Vanessa's going," she said. "She was talking about it in Algebra today. If you went, you could ask her to dance."

"Why do you say things like that? I can't dance, and I wouldn't be caught dead at a mixer. What an idea."

"Your parents would love it if you socialized more," Laurie said. She wanted to be generous to make up for the resentment she sometimes felt toward the boy. "You could go with Jane and me, and hang around with us. We'll talk to Vanessa when we're there. You could just walk up and ask her to dance. Act casual and cool. You know."

"No, I don't know, and neither do you," Will said. "If you knew how to be casual and cool, you wouldn't slobber whenever you see Kai."

"I don't . . ." Laurie looked up at her living-room window and saw her mother watching them. "Smile," she hissed. "I'm not supposed to argue with you."

"Then quit it!" Will said. But he pasted a smile on his face as they turned up the front walk, and Laurie saw her mother smile in response.

"Little creep," she muttered at Will.

"Big tall jerk," he shot back automatically as he waved and grinned at Mrs. Miles.

Their mothers were best friends. Laurie's mother was an artist and Will's was a musician, but their children hadn't inherited their talents. Instead, their best subjects were math and science.

As soon as Laurie and Will walked in the front door, Laurie's mother said, "Will, I've figured out how we can solve the problem you're having with perspective."

Will pulled off his cap and jacket. "Hey, great," he said with forced enthusiasm as he followed Laurie's mother down the hall to her studio. He looked back only once, with crossed eyes and his tongue stuck out.

Vanessa would love that *sight,* Laurie thought, sighing as she picked up Will's jacket and hung it in the hall closet. Then she climbed the steps to her bedroom, wondering how long her homework would take.

Silky, the Siamese cat, watched her from the bed, his blue eyes unblinking.

"Prrrowww?" Silky inquired. He washed one dark paw then glanced up at her again. His eyes were the exact color of Kai's. It unnerved her.

"Don't stare," she told the cat. "Everything is hopeless, and you're only reminding me of it."

He stared anyway.

The biggest problem she had in the entire world was that boy with the cat eyes. That Kai. Even his name was romantic. She didn't have a class with him—he was a junior. She didn't know anybody who could arrange an accidental-on-purpose meeting. And running into him by chance wasn't producing much. It wasn't producing *anything!*

Kai and his family had come from Denmark a few weeks before. So far he had said only six words to Laurie. "Where is the cafeteria, please, miss?"

He'd asked her that in the library on the first day of the new semester. He had a faint accent, just enough for her to know he wasn't American. Although he was blond, his eyebrows and curly eyelashes were black.

Laurie had stared up at him, swallowed hard, and managed to say, "Go to the end of the hall and turn left."

He had nodded politely and walked away. Laurie sagged against her locker and took a deep breath.

"Who is *that?*" Jane, her best friend, asked.

Laurie hadn't known who he was, but she found out that afternoon from Will, while they walked home a block behind the blond boy. The next day she reported to Jane.

"Will says his name is Kai Jensen and he moved into that white house on Crescent Street. He's from Denmark."

"Is there anything in your neighborhood that Will *doesn't* know?" Jane asked. "What did he do, walk up to the Jensens' front door and ask?"

"Actually, yes," Laurie said. "He even gave them the papergirl's phone number."

"Did he find out if this Kai has a girlfriend back in Denmark?" Jane asked.

"Will wouldn't care about that," Laurie had said. "Not at his age."

She still didn't know anything about Kai's personal life. At first, in the school halls, he'd always been alone, but then he began making friends, and she'd seen him with several junior boys. To her relief, she'd never seen him with a girl.

Laurie picked up Silky and sat by her desk. "Valentine's Day is coming," she told him. "Do you care? No, I didn't think you would. You're a boy."

She sighed.

Two days later, on the walk home, Will surprised her. "Remember how we exchanged valentine cards in grade school?" he asked.

"Sure." Rain was falling on the snow and the sidewalk was slippery, so Laurie concentrated on walking. "Mom always made me give a valentine to everybody in class, even the kids I didn't like."

Will snorted. "I had to do that, too. I even had to give cards to the boys who beat me up. But the idea of the whole thing was kind of nice. Well, not really nice, but not too bad, if you see what I mean. You know, putting cards in the big, decorated box. And maybe slipping in a couple that you didn't sign."

Laurie grinned. "Yeah. I did that. I sent 'secret admirer' cards to Peter for three years, and then he figured out that they were from me and tried to kiss me in the locker room and ruined everything."

"Yeah," Will said. "That would ruin everything, all right. Barf."

"Well, it did then, back in fifth grade," Laurie said, vague now because she'd seen Kai ahead of them again, striding along in the rain as if weather never bothered him.

"I've been thinking . . ." Will said. He shrugged.

"You know. About maybe leaving a card in Vanessa's locker."

His words finally sank in and Laurie turned to stare at him. "Are you kidding?"

"Well, maybe yes and maybe no," Will said. "The cracks around the locker doors are big enough to stick stuff inside. I already tried it with a piece of blank paper."

"Somebody would see you do it," Laurie said. "Probably somebody who knows her, and they'd tell her, and then what?"

"I wasn't going to do it at high noon with everybody wandering around the locker room!" Will cried.

"Unless you want her to find out, I recommend that you forget this idea and use the post office."

"It's not the same thing," Will said. "It wouldn't be like putting a secret admirer card in the decorated box in class. We're talking tradition here, Laurie."

"The lockers aren't decorated," Laurie said. "At least, not with anything romantic. And I can guarantee that if you tried decorating her locker with hearts and cupids, she'll stomp on you. Anyway, why are you so hung up on the idea of giving her one of those little cards we used in grade school? The card shop has lots of grown-up cards."

Will scowled, blushed, and looked away. "I know about those other cards. But she might take one of them seriously and think that whoever sent it *could* be a dork, and she'd get mad. But a kid's card, well, she'd probably only laugh and maybe even think it was cute, but it wouldn't be something she had to worry about if she didn't like the guy. See what I mean?"

"I'm trying, Will, but this is not a workable idea."

"I'd wait until after first period starts," Will said. "Nobody's around then. I'll stick the card in her locker and then go to class."

"And be late," Laurie said.

"Oh, who cares about that?" Will exclaimed. "I'm talking about getting the card to her and you're talking about being late. Big deal."

"Okay, don't have a fit. I understand. The card would go in when nobody was around, and then she'd have all day to find it there. That's nice. But what comes next?"

"Another card the next day," Will said. "And the day after that, right up to Valentine's Day."

"And then what?" Laurie asked.

Will gawked at her. "Then nothing! What else could there be?"

"The mixer, you idiot. The mixer."

Will scowled. "I'm not going. I just wanted to do something. . . . Darn it, anyway. I should have known better than to talk to you about this."

"I think it's a terrific idea, but there ought to be some kind of big finish to all this."

"Look what Romeo got when he went for the big finish," Will said, crabby now, his hands shoved in his pockets.

Laurie watched Kai turn the corner and disappear. Rain fell harder.

He's so cute, she thought. *I'd love to send him a valentine every day. The small, old-fashioned ones would be best. Even if he found out I was sending them, he wouldn't get mad. Kids' cards. Hey, it could just be funny, if that was how you wanted to take it. But if you wanted to think they were romantic, you could. I could pick up a box of them and . . . The only problem was delivering them.*

"There's got to be a better way than sneaking around in the locker room every day," Laurie said.

"You could do it for me," Will said. "You're in the same section of the locker room as Vanessa. Nobody would think anything about it if you walked by and sort of absentmindedly went through your pockets to see if you had everything you needed, and then you could stick the valentine in the crack by her door and nobody would see."

"Except Jane," Laurie said. "We always walk together."

"You can't tell her about this!" Will cried. "She'll blab it all over the school."

Laurie shook her head, saying, "No, I won't tell. I won't . . . Hey. I've got an idea."

"What?" Will asked suspiciously.

"If I promise to do it for you—no questions asked about *how* I do it—will you promise to do the same thing for me? As long as we don't end up in the office every morning, waiting for an admittance slip while Mr. Snodgrass watches us through his glass door. He's got eyes like gooseberries and he makes me nervous."

Will stared. "I'm supposed to trust you to do this every day and you won't tell me how?"

"Because I'm not sure yet how I'll manage it," Laurie said. "I'm only promising that I will."

"Why don't you just stand up and hand the card to Vanessa in your algebra class?" Will asked bitterly. "She knows we're neighbors, and maybe she even knows I'm temporarily stuck with you after school while your mother tries to teach me to draw a circle without tracing it around a quarter. Vanessa would figure everything out."

As if it would matter, Laurie thought, feeling more than a little sorry for him. Vanessa was young to be a freshman, but she was still older than Will. And she was taller. She'd probably laugh at him.

All the more reason to keep Will's identity a secret.

"I absolutely promise that she'll never find out who's sending her the cards," she said solemnly. "Trust me."

They were climbing the steps to Laurie's house then, so there wasn't much time left.

"Okay, I guess," Will said. "Remember, you promised."

"And will you promise me the same thing?" Laurie whispered quickly, her hand on the doorknob.

"You want me to get them to Kai?" Will whispered back. "Is that what you're asking?"

Laurie nodded.

The door opened, startling both of them.

"You two look awfully serious," Laurie's mom said.

"I'm helping her with algebra," Will said innocently.

Brat! Laurie thought. "Yes, he was clearing up something for me."

"That's nice," Mom said. "Will, I got out my carving tools. I thought we might try some wood sculpture. I've got a hunch you might be very gifted."

"Great," Will said heartily.

He tossed his jacket to Laurie, nodded significantly to her, and marched off behind Mrs. Miles.

Yes! Laurie thought as she ran upstairs. What a great idea! Kai will never dream it's me and he'll . . .

Silky stared up at her from the middle of the bed.

Laurie sat down beside him abruptly.

"He'll think it's the dumbest thing that ever happened to him," Laurie said aloud.

"Yow," Silky observed, squinting his eyes.

"Oh, what do you know?" Laurie said, laughing, and she rolled Silky over and scratched his stomach while he purred.

The next day, Laurie was digging a notebook out of her locker when she heard someone say, "You live a few blocks away from me."

"What?" Laurie asked. There was a buzzing in her ears, as if bees were swarming around her head.

Kai smiled down at her. "I see you with your friend after school," he said. "You pass the corner where I turn."

"Will's my next-door neighbor," Laurie said, transfixed.

"I know Will," Kai said. "He came to our house after we moved here and told us how to contact the girl who delivers newspapers."

"He told me," Laurie said.

Kai waited a moment, and then asked cautiously, *"What* did he tell you?"

"That he'd gone to see you and told you about Mary Beth Harley," Laurie babbled. The buzzing in her ears was so loud that she wondered if he could hear it. Maybe the racket was what kept him from understanding her.

"Ah," Kai said, nodding. "Now I understand. Will explained that she will start university with him next year, and she is saving the money she earns by delivering papers."

Laurie nodded, completely speechless now.

"May I know your name?" Kai asked.

Laurie gawked at him. "Laurie," she said. She cleared her throat. "I'm Laurie Miles."

The bell for fourth period rang, and Laurie clutched her books to her chest, wondering what to do now.

"Thank you, Laurie," Kai said. "I'll see you again."

He moved away, smiling to himself, and Laurie watched him until he disappeared into the crowd.

"Who was that?" Jane asked as she skidded up behind Laurie. "Was it Kai?"

Laurie nodded.

"Wow," Jane said. "He's ten times cuter up close. Hey, let's go. We'll be late."

Laurie followed her friend obediently. She couldn't stop smiling.

On the way home from school, Laurie and Will detoured past the card store. When they came out, each of them carried a sack containing a box of small valentine cards.

"This is the dumbest thing I ever did," Will said.

"Don't say that," Laurie said. "I'll lose my nerve."

"You didn't tell old big-mouthed Jane, did you?"

"No. It's our secret, yours and mine," Laurie said.

"It better be, considering what I have to put up with from your mother. All my fingers are bandaged, my wood carving of a dog looks like something that hatched out of an underground pod, and my own mother won't rescue me."

"Stop griping," Laurie said. "This time next year, you'll be in college, and I'll still be slogging my way back and forth to high school through rain and snow and . . ."

"I don't want to talk about next year," Will said. "I want to talk about now. How are we going to work this?"

Laurie had thought it through. "I want you to fix a card for Vanessa for every day between now and Valentine's Day and then give them to me."

"I don't want you to read what I write on the inside," Will said. "I'll seal them, and don't get any ideas about steaming them open."

"Try not to be an idiot," Laurie said. "I don't care what you write inside. Just put her name on the outside so she won't think there's been a mistake. I'll do the same thing and we can trade boxes."

"Okay. And I don't care what you write on the inside either," Will said. "But take it from a guy—don't make it too dippy."

Laurie stared at him. "Well, *guy,* I'll do my best."

Alone in her room, with Silky sitting on her desk and watching her print Kai's name on one envelope after another, Laurie had serious doubts about this plan. Kai would probably guess who the cards were from, and he'd think she was too childish to bother with. Or he'd be embarrassed.

She took a deep breath. "But maybe," she said to Silky, "he'd be interested and wonder who was sending them, and be really pleased if he ever found out."

Silky made a small, skeptical sound.

"Well, it *could* turn out that way," Laurie said.

Not likely, Silky seemed to say as he batted Laurie's pen out of her hand. *Quit while you're ahead.*

In spite of the cat, Laurie had the cards and envelopes ready by the time Will showed up after dinner, carrying a notebook and his old algebra book.

"I'm helping Laurie," he told Laurie's dad at the door.

"I didn't know she was having trouble," Laurie's dad said, looking mystified and a little worried.

"I'm not, Dad," Laurie said. "Will, darn you!"

"I was only kidding," Will said. "She's working ahead in the algebra book, and I'll fill in some gaps for her."

"Oh," Dad said, relieved. "Okay, kids, go to it."

"Do you want something to eat?" Mom asked. "Will? We had chocolate pie for dessert, and there's one piece left."

"No, thanks," Will said. Laurie stared at him.

"I don't have forever to do this, Laurie," Will said patiently. "Let's go up to your room and get started."

As they climbed the stairs, Laurie heard Dad say, "He's turning down *pie?* If he doesn't want it, can I have it?"

Once they were inside Laurie's bedroom and the door was shut, Laurie said, "Did you bring the cards?"

"Why else would I be here?" Will opened the notebook and took out a small stack of cards held together with a rubber band. Laurie saw that Vanessa's name was printed in red ink—a nice touch, and one she wished she'd thought of.

"Okay, where are yours?" Will asked.

Laurie took the cards off her desk and handed them to him. "Do you have a plan?" she asked.

"Of course I do," Will said. "But you're better off not knowing."

"What's that supposed to mean?" Laurie asked, worried.

"It means you're better off not knowing," Will said. "Let's sit down and have a look at the book. I hate lying to people. And you could probably use the help anyway."

"I do *not* need help," Laurie said.

"Then let's work ahead in the book," Will said.

"Yow," Silky said thoughtfully. He was looking at the wallpaper as if it contained a secret message.

Afterward, Laurie wondered if maybe the cat *had* been reading a secret message, one that said: "Laurie is about to make a complete idiot of herself."

Will had given her eight cards. She put the first one in her pocket before she left for school that morning. During second period, she developed a coughing fit and slipped out of class for a quick trip to Vanessa's locker—about twenty feet away. She shoved the card into the crack next to the door and practically skipped back to class.

On the way home, Will asked, "Did you do it?"

"Yes. Did you?"

"Yes."

"How?" Laurie asked.

Will glared at her. "Don't ask. But he got it."

Kai wasn't ahead of them that day. Laurie wondered if he'd opened the envelope and dropped dead.

On day two, Laurie coughed and excused herself

from third period, ran down the hall, turned right, stuck the envelope in Vanessa's locker, and ran back. By the time she reached class, she was really coughing.

"What's wrong with you?" Jane whispered.

"I'm coming down with something, I guess," Laurie said. She didn't dare look at Vanessa.

Going home, Will asked, "Did you do it?"

"Did you?"

"I asked first," Will said.

"I delivered it," Laurie said. Ahead of them, Kai strolled with another boy. He didn't look back even once.

On the third day, Laurie coughed in fourth period, and most of the kids in class began laughing.

"Do you need a drink of water?" Ms. Henderson asked.

Laurie nodded and hurried out. Vanessa's locker wasn't far away, but Ms. Clausen, the ugliest and meanest secretary in the office, was scuttling down the hall like a hairy-legged spider, so Laurie had no choice but to stop at the drinking fountain and drink.

Ms. Clausen stopped at a bulletin board, took down a notice, and put up two others.

Laurie went on drinking until Ms. Clausen turned around and stared at her.

Oh, darn, darn! Laurie thought as she went back to class.

"You've dripped water down your front," Jane said when Laurie sat next to her.

"I also slosh when I walk," Laurie said, cranky enough to wish she'd never promised Will to help him with his plan. Now what was she going to do?

She left the next class coughing again, with half

the class coughing behind her—and laughing. She was so far away from Vanessa's locker that it wasn't likely she'd make it there and back without running into somebody.

She sped down the hall, whipped left around the corner—and saw Kai and two other boys coming out of a room.

"Hello, Laurie," he said as he passed her.

She wasn't able to speak. All she could do was cough—all the way to Vanessa's locker and back to class.

That day, walking home, Will said, "I hope things are going okay with you. I mean, I hope you're still on schedule with the cards."

"I haven't missed," Laurie said. "How about you?"

"Done deal," he said.

On Saturday and Sunday, Laurie had no problem delivering the cards. She'd heard Vanessa talking in history class about going away for the weekend with her family. Laurie walked over to Jane's house both days, and detoured an extra block to pass Vanessa's place and put the card inside her storm door. On Sunday, she saw that the card she'd left Saturday was gone, so someone was taking care of their house while they were away.

On Monday, she "forgot" her French grammar book in her locker, and on the way to retrieve it, she delivered another card. During lunch in the cafeteria, Vanessa and two of her friends sat at the next table, and Laurie had to endure listening to the girls speculate about who was leaving the cards in Vanessa's locker.

"I don't know why she's griping," Jane said, keeping her voice low. "If somebody gave me a valentine every day, I'd be happy even if the boy's head came to a point."

Laurie could only shake her head. This was awful! Vanessa was laughing! If Will found out, he'd be devastated.

Of course, Kai was probably laughing with his friends, too.

"I wish I lived on another planet," Laurie said.

"Cheer up," Jane said. "It's only two more days to the mixer, and that ought to be a lot of fun."

Two more days, two more cards, Laurie thought.

Going home, Will asked, "How's everything?"

"Great," Laurie said. "She has every card, and the next two days will be easy."

"How are you doing it?" Will asked.

"How are *you?*"

"Don't ask," Will said.

"Don't you ask either, but you'd better be grateful," Laurie said, remembering how much water she'd had to drink when Ms. Clausen was watching her.

The next morning during first period, Laurie had to go to her locker to get her notebook—and stick the next-to-the-last envelope in Vanessa's locker. But the custodian was cleaning up what looked like spilled soda at that end of the locker room, so Laurie could only get her notebook and return to class. During second period, she wracked her brain trying to think of a reason to leave class, but she couldn't. She couldn't concentrate, either. When the fire alarm rang, she practically jumped out of her skin.

"Wouldn't you know they'd wait until it's raining to have a fire drill?" Jane grumbled as they lined up.

Maybe, Laurie thought, she could find a way to slip the envelope in Vanessa's locker when the drill was over and nobody was paying attention to who stayed in line. She checked her pocket to make sure the envelope was still there. Yes. But she'd have to get rid of Jane. How?

They were outside, waiting in the drizzle for the drill to end, when she saw Kai across the campus from her.

What did he think of the cards? Did he want to find out who sent them? Or did he wish the person would stop? Was he telling his friends and laughing, like Vanessa?

The drill was over. Laurie and Jane hurried toward the door, damp and shivering.

"I want to stop by my locker," Laurie said. "I'm cold and I want my jacket."

"Me, too," Jane said. "Oh, look. Everybody else has the same idea. I'll meet you back in class."

What a break. Laurie got her jacket quickly, then walked toward Vanessa's locker, trying to seem as if she was waiting for somebody. She didn't see Vanessa, but one of her friends passed by and smiled. Laurie got the envelope out of her pocket and held it inside her jacket. There was the locker. All she had to do was walk slowly and push the envelope in the crack as she passed.

It dropped to the floor.

Now what? There were too many people around, and somebody would see her pick it up. Should she leave it?

It had landed face up, but that didn't mean Vanessa or any of her friends would see it. Laurie snatched it up and went back to class, all the while expecting someone behind her to yell, "Hey, what did you pick up?"

And she was still stuck with the original problem, getting the card to Vanessa.

She managed to deliver the envelope during lunch break, by telling Jane she wasn't very hungry and wanted to return a book to the school library. "Get me a dessert, and I'll meet you at our table," she told Jane.

The locker room was jammed with so many kids that she could hope no one would notice when she passed Vanessa's locker and tried the same thing again. But her heart was hammering when she hurried away, mission accomplished.

I can't stand doing this even one more time, she thought. *It's dumb. Vanessa's laughing at it, and that would hurt Will's feelings. Kai's probably laughing, too. . . . But I can't tell Will I want to stop. I've only got one more envelope. . . . I'll throw it out and tell him I delivered it. What's the difference? Seven valentines are just as good as eight.*

When she sat down at the table, Jane handed her a plastic carton of chocolate pudding. "It was this or something they're calling "orange crumble," but it looked left over from last year and the crumble part was all gummy."

"Thank you for ruining my appetite for a million years," Laurie said. She was watching Vanessa, who was listening to what one of her friends was telling her. She nodded and laughed, and Laurie wondered if they were talking about the cards.

Will's mother picked him up after school to take him to the dentist. Laurie crossed the street, hoping to see Kai ahead of her. And there he was.

But he wasn't walking. He was waiting.

For her?

She looked down, certain he was waiting for

someone else. But as she passed him, he said, "Laurie?"

She looked up. He smiled a little, and seemed nervous.

"Yes?" she asked, panicked.

"May I walk with you?" he asked. "I see that your neighbor isn't here."

"He had to go to the dentist," Laurie said. Her voice sounded strange. Did he think so, too?

He fell into step with her, hands in his pockets, looking straight ahead.

The silence was too much. "Do you like living here?" Laurie asked.

"Yes." He hesitated, glanced down at her and then away. "But I don't understand all of your customs."

"Which customs?" Laurie asked.

But he didn't answer right away. "I've made some friends," he said. "They explained many things. But for some things, I think I should ask a girl."

"Like what?" Laurie asked nervously.

He sighed and pushed his hair away from his forehead. "Every morning the girl who delivers our newspaper has been including an envelope with my name on it."

"What?" Laurie gasped. Darn Will anyway! He hadn't been delivering the cards! He'd somehow talked Mary Beth into doing it for him.

Kai looked sorrowful. "You are surprised," he said. "So am I. My parents and I are not familiar with cards like these, cards with little animals asking, 'Be my valentine.' But we think it applies to the St. Valentine's Day holiday you celebrate."

He'd told his parents! Oh, Laurie thought wildly, she was going to kill Will the next time she saw him.

"The kids here exchange cards in grade school,"

Laurie said, trying to sound as if she was only offering him information that had nothing to do with her.

"But the girl who brings our papers is a senior," Kai said. "Why would she do this? Why doesn't she sign the cards? She draws small hearts with arrows stuck on them."

Laurie wanted to run—and keep running until she was a hundred miles away. "You can see those hearts all over school, on the posters for the Valentine's Day mixer."

"My friends explained the mixer," Kai said. "But not the hearts."

"I guess they thought you'd know," Laurie said.

"Valentine's Day is a new holiday for me," Kai said. "We don't have it in Denmark."

Laurie could have cried. Or screamed. Why hadn't she thought of that? Just because Americans made a big deal out of Valentine's Day didn't mean Europeans did.

"My mother says I must send Mary Beth a thank you card," Kai said.

"No, no, no!" Laurie cried.

"I beg your pardon?" Kai asked, startled.

How could she explain without incriminating herself? "Look," she said finally, "if the cards don't have a name on them, that means the sender wants it to be a secret."

"But I see her deliver the paper every morning before breakfast," he said. He was obviously baffled.

Laurie bent her head and hunched her shoulders. Everything was hopeless. "Don't write her a thank-you note," she said. "You'd embarrass her."

"But don't the cards require an answer?" he

asked. "I am not certain what she wants when she asks me to be her valentine. Is that another word for boyfriend?"

"No," Laurie said, weary now. "It's just a way that little kids tell other little kids that they're going to be good friends for a long time."

"Ah." Kai smiled. His blue eyes lit up. "I can do that. I can tell her we'll be friends."

"No, no, don't do that either," Laurie said. "Don't do anything at all."

"But . . ." Kai began.

"I've got to go home," Laurie said.

"I'll walk with you," Kai said. "I am enjoying our conversation."

I'm not, Laurie thought wildly. *I hate this!*

"We can talk about American customs," Kai said. He took long steps, and she had to hurry to keep up.

Afterward, she couldn't remember what they'd talked about. She was too nervous to make sense, and she was grateful when he said good-bye at the corner where he usually turned off.

Will Storey, she thought savagely as she hurried home. *I'll deliver that last card for you. And I'll write your name and address on the envelope!*

Will phoned her that night after dinner and whispered, "There's one card left."

"I know that," she said. She fantasized about how large she would print his name on that card.

"Kai will get his last card tomorrow morning," Will said.

Laurie looked around to make certain her parents were too far away to hear.

"Listen, you little creep," she hissed into the phone. "I found out how you've been delivering the cards. You want to hear how I know? Kai asked me if he should write Mary Beth a thank-you note! He thinks *she's* sending these cards. What did you tell her? Is she laughing at me? Is everybody laughing?"

"Nobody's laughing!" Will said. "Get a grip on yourself, will you? I paid Mary Beth five whole dollars to do this, and I told her she couldn't ask questions or even *think* about who was sending the cards, and she agreed."

"She's probably crazy about him," Laurie fumed. "She's probably going to take credit for this—if he ends up liking the whole thing. Or she'll blame me if he hates it."

"She won't!" Will said. "She's got a boyfriend. Why don't you wake up and pay attention to what's going on around school, Laurie?"

"Oh, I'm awake, all right," Laurie snarled. "If anything else goes wrong, you'd better look out. I'll tell Mom that you want to learn to make pottery!"

"Laurie . . ." Will began.

Laurie hung up.

The next day, before Jane arrived and even before she went to her own locker, Laurie delivered the last of Will's valentines. In spite of her anger, she didn't write Will's name on the envelope. She'd keep her word even if he had betrayed her.

The mixer would be that afternoon after school, and most of the girls wore red. Laurie, who would rather have gone to the doctor for shots, knew she was in for the worst time of her life.

And to make everything ridiculous, Mary Beth, who might have been the smartest girl in school but still managed to dress like her own grandmother most of the time, walked by wearing a gorgeous white sweater and red skirt, and she'd had her hair cut in a cute new style. Kai was going to ask her to dance and thank her for the cards, and she'd probably take credit for them, too, even if she did have a boyfriend.

"Gee, you look crabby," Jane said as she skidded up, out of breath.

"I *am* crabby," Laurie said.

"Well, cheer up. You look cute in that shirt, and we're going to have a great time at the mixer today."

Laurie groaned. "I think I'm coming down with something, maybe even the bubonic plague. I'll probably go straight home after school."

"Hello, Laurie."

Kai strolled by with a friend. He wore a red sweater over a white shirt, and he looked so wonderful that Laurie felt like cheering. She smiled instead.

"I'll see you at the mixer this afternoon," he said.

She couldn't get out a word.

He looked disappointed. As he walked away, he glanced back at her over his shoulder.

"He likes you," Jane said. "I can tell. Why are you treating him like that?"

Laurie stuck her key in her locker and twisted it. "I ought to have my head examined," she said. "I'm absolutely certain that I've gone crazy. I just wish you'd mentioned it to me before I made such an idiot out of myself."

A small, square envelope fell out of her locker when she pulled the door open.

"Hey, what's that?" Jane asked as she bent down. "It's got your name on it."

Laurie took the envelope out of Jane's hand. Her ears were buzzing again. Was this one of Will's jokes? The envelope was exactly like the ones she'd made out for Kai, exactly like the ones she'd been stuffing in Vanessa's locker.

"Gosh, that looks like the kind of cards Vanessa's been getting," Jane said. "Open it and find out who sent it."

Laurie's fingers felt clumsy, almost numb. She tore open the envelope, pulled out the card, and saw a drawing of a small, brown teddy bear dressed in a red jacket who smiled and asked, "Be My Valentine, Valentine?"

She opened the card. Inside, someone had drawn a heart with an arrow through it.

"That's so cute," Jane said. "I wish I had a secret admirer. I love that, Laurie! You and Vanessa are lucky."

"She doesn't think so," Laurie said.

"Maybe yes, maybe no," Jane said. "Don't you remember how we always acted in grade school? We always pretended we hated the cards that didn't have names. But we really loved getting them. And we loved guessing who'd sent them."

"I don't need to guess about this one," Laurie said. "Will did this, I bet. Just to make me mad."

Jane took the envelope. "That's awfully nice handwriting for somebody who's twelve."

Laurie stuffed her jacket in the locker and slammed the door shut. "He's not going to grow any older, that's for sure," she said.

"Don't do anything to scare him," Jane said. "We're still letting him go to the mixer with us, aren't we? I think that's so cute. Don't pick on him, Laurie."

"He'll *wish* I'd only picked on him," Laurie muttered.

The day dragged on forever. Twice, Laurie saw Will in the distance, but when she attempted to catch up with him, he disappeared into the crowd.

In algebra, Vanessa giggled and whispered throughout class. She'd changed her mind about the valentine cards, it seemed. Now she wondered aloud if the boy sending them would show up at the mixer.

"Frannie said she saw a boy hanging around my locker yesterday," Vanessa said. "But she couldn't tell for sure who it was."

"Maybe he'll ask you to dance this afternoon," Jane said.

"Maybe he won't," Vanessa said. "I wouldn't. I'd be scared that I'd get turned down."

"Good grief, what does Will see in her?" Laurie grumbled under her breath. "Idiot."

During lunch break, she found a very small stuffed bear hanging from her locker door. He wore a red sweater.

"Laurie's got a boyfriend, Laurie's got a boyfriend," a freshman boy chanted as he walked past.

"Grow up, Craig," Laurie cried. She untied the ribbon that held the bear in place and shoved the little animal into her skirt pocket.

Who was doing this? Was it Will's crazy idea? What was the point?

When she came back to the locker after her lunch break, another bear hung there. This one wore a red skirt and had a tiny bow between its ears.

"Aww," Jane said. "Look at that! Isn't it sweet?"

Laurie shoved the bear in her other pocket and looked around. Who was responsible?

"I bet it's Kai," Jane said. "I bet he's the one doing this."

Laurie blushed so hard her face hurt. "No, he thinks Mary Beth likes him."

"How do you know?" Jane demanded. "Why would he think something like that?"

Laurie sighed. "I can't tell you now, but I will tonight. It's the dumbest story you'll ever hear."

"Oh, good," Jane said. "I love dumb stories, especially if they happened to somebody else. Come on, cheer up. We've only got two hours to go until the mixer."

"Wonderful," Laurie said crossly. "I can hardly wait."

After school, Will was nowhere in sight. Laurie couldn't find him in any of his usual hangouts, and when she and Jane reached the gym where the mixer was being held, she didn't see him there, either. He'd done what he'd threatened to do, and avoided it altogether.

"Coward," Laurie muttered to herself.

If she'd really wanted revenge, she would have had it when she saw Vanessa mooning around by the snack table, wondering who had sent her the cards and where he was. Will was missing his chance, and it served him right.

But then again, maybe Vanessa would have been stunned to find the twelve-year-old was her secret admirer.

Maybe, Laurie thought as she helped herself to a can of soda, *maybe it's better to keep a big distance between fantasies and reality, and not hope for anything.*

As far as Jane's theory about who had given her the little bears—well, Laurie had her own suspicions about that. Kai probably didn't know American girls collected stuffed animals, either. The bears were from somebody absolutely awful, and he'd show up in a minute and want to dance, right out there in the middle of the floor with everybody—including Kai—watching.

But Kai wasn't there, either.

"Have a sandwich," Jane said. "I don't see any freshmen dancing. Maybe we should go home."

Laurie put down her soft drink. "Then let's," she said. "I'll tell you what's been going on, and you can laugh all you want. Somebody ought to be happy today."

They were halfway to the door when Kai and his friend came in. Kai saw her immediately and walked toward her.

Her ears began buzzing.

Kai handed her a pink rosebud tied with a pink ribbon. "Happy Valentine's Day," he said. "Will you dance with me?"

Laurie blinked. "I thought you weren't coming."

He smiled. "I had to go home to get the rose."

She looked down at the rose and then up at him. "I . . ." she began, and then she ran out of words.

"It's a tradition," he said. "Mary Beth told me. I had to ask her, because you didn't tell me, and I don't know any other girls. She explained roses and teddy bear collections to me."

"And the cards?" Laurie asked in a small, scared voice.

"Ah, the cards," Kai said. "They will remain a mystery forever. Mary Beth said she has taken an oath to keep the secret. And so has her boyfriend, who delivered one of the cards when Mary Beth stayed home because she was ill. So, Laurie, will you dance with me?"

Laurie held out her hand and smiled when he took it.

Once, when Laurie was dancing with Kai that afternoon, she saw Will peeking in the door. He wasn't watching her. He watched Vanessa, sitting at a table with her girlfriends, devouring sandwiches. Will looked oddly satisfied, and why not? His secret was still a secret.

"I like your smile," Kai said. "What were you thinking about?"

"I was thinking about cards and bears and roses," Laurie said.

"So was I. You have interesting traditions."

Does he know? she wondered. *I hope so.*

"I'm glad you like us," she said. "Very glad."

Jean Thesman

Valentine's Day has always been one of my favorite holidays, in spite of my spectacularly bad luck when I was sixteen. A shy boy I liked a lot asked me to a formal Valentine dance. A serious storm came up and our power went out while I was dressing. Our house was hard to find and Jack had never been there. An hour after he was supposed to pick me up, my dad looked out the window and told me there was a suspicious black car parked across the street. (To Dad, any car picking me up was suspicious.) I went out to see if it was Jack. It was. He'd been there for most of the hour, watching the house and wondering if we were home or if I'd stood him up. I suddenly realized that this cute boy was an extremely dim bulb. The whole neighborhood was dark! What did he think had happened?

I invited him inside to get warm, and while he was crossing the small footbridge over a little creek, he missed his footing and slipped in, up to his knees in cold water. He sat in miserable silence by the fire Dad had built, with his shoes and socks off. My parents and I talked among ourselves for what seemed to be forever.

Finally the power blinked back on. Jack was asleep. He had corn plasters on four of his toes.

My father said, "I never did think girls should be allowed to pick their own dates," and Jack woke up, startled, yelling, "What? What?"

"See?" Dad said disgustedly.

My mother was almost hysterical, trying not to laugh. Our dog, who finally noticed that a stranger was in the house, wouldn't stop barking. He was especially interested in the corn plasters.

Dad put a stop to everything by declaring that it was too late to go out. Jack left, and we never spoke to each other again. Dad told this story a million times, using it as an example of how I was drawn to idiots, and Mom always referred to Jack as, "That poor boy with the bad feet."

So much for romance.

JEAN THESMAN is the author of more than a dozen books for young people, including *The Rain Catchers.* She lives near Seattle with her husband and several dogs.

Duet
(A Valentine's Day story)

Kathryn Jensen

January 28

Chaz ran to the mailbox, frantically brushed off the snow, and shoved his hand down inside the metal box. "It has to be here today," he mumbled, feeling his pulse throb in his throat when he tried to swallow.

"What has to be here?" Brian elbowed their friend Randy out of his way so he could see into the mouth of the box.

"Wendy's letter."

"Didn't she just write you a few days ago?"

"A week, it's been a whole week . . . eight days to be exact." Chaz pulled out a fistful of envelopes and flipped through them. "Bill . . . bill . . . advertisement . . . bill . . . coupons . . ."

"What's wrong with a week?" Randy asked.

"We promised we'd write every day when she moved to Baltimore."

Chaz caught the look Brian flashed at Randy. The two of them turned away, grinning.

"Listen," Chaz said, stuffing the mail into his jacket pocket, "you guys can think anything you like. The fact is, Wendy was . . . *is* the prettiest, sexiest girl that ever walked the halls of East Chicago Senior High, and she sounds better than half the female singers with recording contracts."

"So you were interested in her just for business

purposes, for the band," Brian stated solemnly. "For Blue Fusion."

"Of course not. We were . . . *are* going together." Chaz strode toward the front door and stormed through it, tossing the pile of mail on the kitchen table beside his little sister's black-and-white stuffed Guernsey cow. Other kids carried around teddy bears and Barbie dolls; Tilly liked cows. Go figure.

"Hard to date a pretty girl . . . who's a thousand miles away," Brian sang to the melody of a song they'd been practicing all week.

"Baltimore isn't a thousand miles from Chicago," Chaz said impatiently.

"Pretty close," Randy pointed out, grabbing an apple from the glass bowl on the table and biting into it. "Might as well be a million for all the good it will do Blue Fusion."

"Or *you,"* Brian added. "Sorta hard to kiss a girl over the phone."

Chaz ran a hand through his short, blond hair and glared at his two friends. Why wouldn't they give it a rest? He felt sick to his stomach and restless. If Wendy had been there, they'd have all been down in the basement, working on a new song for the gig coming up that Saturday. She'd be singing in her clear, sweet voice, dreamy words of love, and looking at him . . . *at him* . . . her blue eyes sparkling. He'd run his fingers over the keys of the Kawai, his music weaving with hers, working magic in his heart.

He could see her so clearly in his mind, swinging her long, honey-gold hair as she bent over the microphone cupped between her hands, her eyes softly closed in concentration. He could imagine the words rippling from her pretty pink lips. More than anything in the world, he ached to reach out and hold her. He missed Wendy so much . . . and now another day had passed with no letter.

"Hey, Chaz, don't take it so hard, man," Brian said, his voice no longer teasing. "Look at it this way, now you can date other girls. You don't have to be tied down to one."

"Yeah," Randy agreed, tossing his apple core into the trash can under the sink, "like every time we play, there's groupies hanging all over you. Now you can take advantage of the situation."

Chaz shrugged. "The attention is nice," he admitted. "But after a while, it gets kind of old. Wendy and I . . . we were just right for each other. We understood our music and made it happen."

Brian laid a hand on his shoulder. "Well, we've got to make it happen without her now, so you'd better shake it off. Remember, we have to play at the Dust Bin this Saturday. I asked Sandy Ross to come to practice today."

"Why?" Chaz asked, confused. Sandy had been in a couple of musicals at school, but she wasn't a band performer.

"Because we need a girl singer, that's why—duh! Sandy's the best I could dig up on short notice. Come on, let's go downstairs and warm up. She'll be here soon. I gave her the charts this morning. Even if she's had time to work alone on the songs, she'll need to go over them a bunch of times with us to get it together."

Chaz nodded, knowing Brian was right even though his heart wasn't in practicing.

* * *

That night, around 8:00, it started to snow again. Chaz moved his keyboard up from the basement to his bedroom and set up the stand near the window overlooking Bentley Street. He worked on a new song he'd been composing. *For Wendy,* he'd written at the top of the sheet of lined staff paper.

He watched the snow drift down gracefully through the lemon glow of a streetlight. His mom had cranked up the heat when the temperature dropped below twenty degrees. After half an hour of hard playing, Chaz was sweating. He cracked open his window to let a sliver of chill air into the room. It smelled like snow—clean and crisp. He reached out, caught white flakes on his hand and drew them inside, then watched them melt on his palm.

Gone. They were gone that quickly . . . just like Wendy. His Wendy.

February 1

No matter how much homework Chaz had, or how long he practiced the new arrangements for that Saturday, he made time each night to write Wendy a short letter. Sandy wasn't anywhere near as good as Wendy had been; her vocal range was limited and she sang in a different key. In his letters, Chaz told Wendy how frustrating it was working with the new singer. Transposing had always been difficult for him, but he had to rewrite all of the charts by Saturday and make sure everyone knew his part. If the band messed up in the middle of a gig, they might not get paid. They might even lose future jobs.

That night, he had trouble concentrating. All he could see was Wendy's face. Chaz's glance fell to the large black lump of fur at his feet. "Why isn't she writing, Rush?"

The black Labrador, who no longer seemed to match the name Chaz had given him as a puppy, lazily rolled his eyes up to observe him.

"I know, I know . . . getting used to a new school is hard. She's probably busy trying to make new friends, help her mom unpack, and catch up on classwork . . . that sort of stuff."

He sighed. Rush sighed, too.

"Last letter, she said she was crying while she wrote it. Maybe writing makes her so sad she can't do it."

He looked down at Rush, who had closed his eyes as if he'd lost interest in the conversation.

"Of course, there are other ways to keep in touch." Chaz looked at the telephone, then remembered his father's warning.

"I'm not dishing out hundreds of dollars for you to chat long distance with your girlfriend. Any calls to Baltimore that show up on my bill—they're your responsibility."

"Yes, sir," Chaz murmured now as he picked up the receiver. Before he'd finished punching in the last two numbers, his heart was singing happily in his chest. He anticipated Wendy's voice, could imagine how pleased she'd sound when she realized it was him.

The jangling sound cut off in the middle of the third ring, and the Renslers' answering machine picked up. Chaz listened, disappointed but also reassured to find they'd kept the same tape Wendy had recorded for their machine in Chicago. Listening to her voice, even though it was just a recording, made him feel as if she were still just around the corner, in the old brick house where he'd visited her so often.

The machine beeped at him.

"Hi!" he said brightly, then couldn't think of anything else to say. "I . . . well, of course you know this is Chaz. Miss you. Love you." He stared around the room. "Um . . . we're playing on Saturday at the Dust Bin. You know, that club downtown you always wanted to do but we couldn't get a booking. Well, it was your singing on the demo tape that cinched the deal. Now they'll have to settle for second best. Like I said in my letters, Brian got us another singer, but she's not that hot." He didn't want to stop talking, even if it was just to her machine. "Hey," he whispered, "I really miss you a lot, Wen. Wish I could see you or—"

The machine clicked off, and a second later the dial tone buzzed in his ear. Slowly, Chaz put down the receiver. He stayed up until after 1:00 AM, hoping Wendy would call back. But she didn't.

February 2

"Cha-a-a-a-z!"

"What is it this time, Tilly?" he shouted up the stairs from the basement, where Blue Fusion was rehearsing.

"Rush has something in his mouth and he won't give it back!"

Brian laughed. "That dog of yours is a born kleptomaniac."

"He just steals stuff to get attention," Chaz commented, erasing the penciled-in notes he'd made on the sheet music.

"Maybe you should go see what it is," Randy mumbled. He adjusted two knobs on his amp and produced a squealing reverb. "Cool." He grinned. "Retro sixties! Seriously, I mean, what if it's a check or something important for your Mom or Dad—"

"Chaz!" Tilly wailed from the kitchen.

Chaz shook his head but didn't get up from the bench in front of his board. "She's probably upset because it's something of hers. Like that dumb cow."

Tilly appeared at the top of the stairs and glared down at him, her hands propped on her hips. "Well, if you don't want your stupid old letter, I don't care what Rush does to it."

Chaz shot to his feet and raced up the stairs in threes. "Where is he?" he shouted, brushing past his sister.

"He ran upstairs."

"*Now* he decides to run," Chaz muttered. "Rush! Rush, you come back here with that!"

Of course, whatever the mutt had snatched could have been any kind of envelope, for anyone in the family. He wouldn't put it past Tilly to intentionally aggravate him by letting on the letter was from Wendy when she had no idea what it was. But something heavy and painful weighing down the bottom of his stomach made him sure that, of all the junk mail Rush could have gobbled up, he was now chomping on Wendy's letter. The first letter from her in two weeks.

As he tore through the house after the dog, he thought about Wendy's soft hands drawing her lavender pen across the sheets of pale pink stationery, leaving fat, swirling letters of purple ink—and a wave of warmth spread through him. He suspected the letter would be a long one. She'd have saved up so much news for him, and she'd have to tell him over and over again how much she missed him. Maybe she'd just written a little bit each night, curled up in bed with the lamp beside her bed glowing across her pretty face. Then she'd put all the pages together into one envelope and sent them to him.

He hoped Rush hadn't already licked off all the perfume. He loved the rose-petal scent of Wendy's letters.

Chaz ran into his parents' room first. That was where Rush usually hid when he knew he'd been bad. But there was no sign of him there. Swerving around, Chaz looped back down the hallway. Tilly's door was closed; Rush didn't know how to shut doors behind himself. The bathroom was too small to hide the big black dog, and Chaz could see right into it. That left his own room.

He dashed into it. A canine backside crouched low on the carpet, tail wagging. The front half of the body and head had disappeared beneath the bedspread, which hung off the foot of the bed. Rush couldn't see Chaz, so he must have thought Chaz couldn't see him.

"Fork it over, wise guy!" Chaz shouted.

A pitiful whine escaped from beneath the bed. Rush's tail altered from wag mode to thump mode.

"I said, give it to me!" Chaz demanded. By now the envelope would be covered with dog drool. If it were from Wendy, he hoped she'd used waterproof ink.

Chaz reached under the fringe of the spread, grabbed Rush's leather collar, and hauled him out from under the bed. He snatched the envelope out of the dog's jaws, but a tearing sound told him he'd been too hasty.

"Oh, no," he moaned, holding up the jagged pink paper square.

It definitely was a letter from Wendy, and a good third of it had torn away. Chaz glared at Rush, who smacked his huge jaws twice then, with a satisfied roll of his eyes, swallowed. Rush sat proudly grinning at him, as if to say, "See, I win after all."

Chaz collapsed in disgust on the bed. Resting his wide head on his master's knee, Rush gazed up at him adoringly.

"You sure pick great ways to show your affection," Chaz said, stroking the soft black fur on his dog's head. "I just hope there's enough of this to bother reading."

Chaz pried open the flap on the envelope, aware that it seemed a lot thinner than he'd expected it to be. He pulled out a single page of pink stationary, rosebuds trailing across the top. Smiling, Chaz started to read.

It didn't matter that a strip down one side was missing and the last part beneath the bottom fold was so blurry from dog saliva he could barely make out the words. What was important was that Wendy had written to him—because she loved him. She must have had a good reason for taking so long to get back to him. Their separation had to be even harder on her than it was for him. After all, he'd gotten to stay in Chicago with all of their old friends. She was facing a city full of strangers and scary adjustments to a new school, strange neighborhood, and a house that, she'd written, had totally freaked her out, it was so big and empty.

Feeling a lump of sympathy grow in his throat, he began reading:

Dear Chaz,

Sorry I didn't get a chance to call you back the other night. My dad is being a real boring jerk about long distance phone calls. He says if he lets me call my old friends, in Chicago, he'll have to let my sisters call their friends too. That's totally unfair. Lainy and Jennifer aren't even in high school. Like, how important can friends be when you're only twelve years old?

Anyway, yes, I still miss you. I've decided that I can't
down. After all, as close as we have been, we both know
together for always. Don't you agree?

I'm sure the new singer Brian got for the ba
Is she very pretty? Does she have a nice voi
madly in love with her? Just teasing.

As for me, I'v
so cool and plays
every night

So, I guess
next summer maybe
Dad says we can visit then. If you

Still singing,
Wendy

Chaz sighed and crushed the letter to his chest. He wished he'd gotten it away from Rush before the stupid mutt chewed off most of the right side, but at least he could figure out most of what Wendy was saying. He knew her so well it wasn't hard to guess. She missed him; she'd said that much. And she must have had one heck of a fight with her dad over using the phone. She'd probably cried most of the night when her father wouldn't let her call him back.

Chaz chuckled to himself, thinking he really

shouldn't be so pleased that she'd been upset. But it made him feel good to know she still cared about him. "Together for always." He read the words from her letter over and over, and they melted his heart. Yes, that was it—Wendy and Chaz. Always.

As for the rest of the note, he was pretty sure what she'd been thinking. She was jealous of Sandy, their new singer, probably worried he would fall for her. Well, he wouldn't, not a chance. Wendy was the only girl for him. And even though some of the words were missing, she must have said something about thinking of him "every night." Just like he thought of her. She was already talking about their spending the summer together.

Chaz's pulse raced at the thought. Now that was a great idea! Once they were out of school for summer vacation, there was no reason for her to stay in Baltimore or for him to remain in Chicago. They could get jobs in one place or the other, so that they'd be together. If she came back to Chicago, they could work days, waiting on tables in a fancy restaurant on Lake Shore Drive or inside the Loop, where tips from tourists were good. At night, Wendy would sing with the band. Maybe he could even line up a few gigs for Blue Fusion at Shelter or Cabaret Metro, two of the hottest clubs in the city.

He felt excited just thinking about the possibilities. But then . . . summer was a long way off.

February 4

"You're going *where?*" Brian gasped.

"I'm going to Baltimore," Chaz announced, "to surprise Wendy for Valentine's Day."

Brian and Randy stared at him as if he were crazy.

"Hey, it's no big deal," Chaz insisted. "It'll be cool. I'll buy her a cheesy card and some chocolates and roses, show up at her door with them. She'll go nuts!"

"She already is nuts," Randy grumbled, "getting involved with you. What about the band?"

"What about it?" Chaz asked, cheerfully. "I'll only be gone for a few days. A week at the most, if her parents invite me to stay for a longer visit."

"What about your folks?" Brian asked.

Chaz shrugged. "My dad enlisted in the Navy when he was eighteen, not much older than I am." He frowned, thinking about the discussion he'd had with his father the night before. "Only trouble is, he won't let me take his car, and I have to pay my own expenses. And no hitching rides—has to be public transportation."

"So, how are you going to get there?"

"Fly!" Chaz exclaimed with a grin. "What other way is there?"

Chaz hung up the phone. "Three hundred forty-two dollars," he muttered, stunned by the figure.

"What?" Tilly asked.

"That's the best rate I could get for round-trip air fare between Chicago and Baltimore. What a crock!" He sat down at the kitchen table and wrote the figure on a pad of paper. "I have almost a hundred now. After we play on Saturday night, I'll have another fifty. But I have to buy the flowers—a dozen roses, that's about fifty bucks right there. Then there are the chocolates—that's at least another fifteen if I get a heart-shaped box of the good stuff. Five bucks for a big lacy job of a card . . ."

"That's seventy," Tilly chimed in helpfully.

"I can add," Chaz snapped.

"You aren't going far on thirty dollars." Why did she have to be such a whiz at math?

"Eighty, after Saturday's gig," he mumbled.

Tilly looked at him across the kitchen table, her green eyes suddenly too serious for an eight-year-old. "Don't you think you should call Wendy and tell her you're coming?" She stroked her stuffed cow. If she pulled the string under its chin it would let out a long, plaintive *moooooo.* It was the dumbest thing Chaz had ever seen.

"That'd spoil the surprise, bubble head."

Tilly shrugged. "How will you get from the airport to her house if she doesn't pick you up?"

Chaz considered that for a second. "Good thinking. A taxi. I'd better figure on another twenty bucks." He studied the numbers. With less than two weeks to Valentine's Day, he didn't have much time to save. The most he could hope for was another hundred bucks; he'd still be short.

If it had been summer, things might have been easier. He could have hauled the Kawai down to Grant Park and played for tips from the passing tourists. You could pick up a cool hundred on a sunny Saturday, if you hammed it up for the crowd. But it was the middle of winter. Snow covered the ground. Few people strolled along the water's edge for pleasure. Hunched over against the icy blasts off Lake Michigan, people scuttled around like beetles in search of warm holes.

After school that day, Chaz dropped in at a bunch of clubs in the Loop, a section of downtown Chicago favored by college kids and other seekers of night life. He asked managers if he could play on weekdays for tips. Two agreed to let him.

Chaz knocked himself out, pounding the Kawai for four hours straight at Donovan's that night. The next evening, he played in an experimental jazz club called Weeds, without a break until after eleven. But the crowds during the middle of the week were thin, and the people who did show up didn't seem to have much spending money after Christmas. He came away with twenty-three dollars the first night and only fifteen the next.

The following day, he talked Brian into letting him come with him to work at Burger Palace, where they talked the manager into letting him fill in for one of his regular cashiers who hadn't shown up. He went again the next day. At $4.50 an hour, for six hours, he made more than he'd earned at the bars, but then his cash register came up short by ten dollars.

"Sorry, it'll have to come out of your pay," the manager told him.

"Well, it's at least seventeen dollars I didn't have before."

"Sure," the man said. "That's the way to look at it." He waved them toward the door, the key in his hand. "See you tomorrow, Brian."

"What about me?" Chaz asked.

"You can fill in for my no-shows any time you like," the manager said.

"I mean, my money."

"You'll get your check on the fifteenth of the month like everyone else."

"The fifteenth . . . of February?" Chaz nearly choked. He stared at Brian.

"I didn't even think about that," his friend admitted. "No one gets paid cash these days, except for musicians."

Chaz felt sick to his stomach. He'd wasted two whole days, and wouldn't see the money for his hard work until after he returned from Baltimore.

February 8

Chaz prayed for a blizzard. A guy could make good money shoveling snow for neighbors. But the weather remained dry, although it was miserably cold and windy. People stayed indoors. At the Dust Bin that Saturday night, only a few people ventured onto the dance floor, and more than half of the tables were empty. The bartender cornered Chaz and Brian at 11:00, after Blue Fusion's first set.

"Guys, I don't think we're going to clear much at the door tonight. Afraid I'll have to let you go early."

Chaz's heart leapt into his throat. "You're still going to pay us what we agreed, right?"

"How can I pay you what I don't take in?" the man asked. "I should have cancelled completely after last night's low turnout. The place is dead again tonight. Hey, at least you're going away with enough to cover your gas and put a few extra bucks in your pocket."

They split up the cash in the car. Chaz got twenty-five dollars instead of the fifty he'd counted on. He felt as if he were losing money instead of gaining it.

Early the next morning, he walked door to door around the neighborhood, asking people if they had any odd jobs to be done around their houses. He picked up another twenty dollars cleaning out a garage for an elderly couple. But that was the only work he could find. It was too early for spring cleaning, and yard work would have to wait for the ground to thaw.

The next night, although it was during the middle of a week, Blue Fusion was booked to play in a small bar close to the University of Chicago campus. But during practice that same afternoon, the main amp died.

"There's nothing we can do but buy a new one, and fast," Brian solemnly informed the group.

Randy shook his head. "Even if we can find a used one on short notice, it's going to run us three or four hundred."

Chaz stared at him, feeling empty inside . . . as empty as his wallet was going to become in the next twenty-four hours. "We have to play. If we don't show, they'll never book us again. And word will get around we're unreliable."

"But you need to hold on to your trip money," Randy pointed out, looking worried. He strummed his guitar, producing a flat twang.

"We don't have a choice." Chaz swallowed over the jagged lump in his throat. "We have to all chip in and buy that amp. There's no other way."

That night, after they'd played, Chaz tried calling Wendy again, but her mother answered. "I'm sorry, Chaz, Wendy's not here now. I'll mention to her that you called. Tell me how things are going back in Chicago—we miss the old neighborhood."

Chaz talked to Mrs. Rensler for just a few minutes, then told her he had to do homework even though he didn't have any. Paying long-distance charges to talk to Wendy was one thing. Handing cash over to his dad to pay for talking to her mother was something else.

He wrote another letter to Wendy, but kept his surprise travel plans to himself. When they were together, he'd tell her about all the crazy things he'd done to earn money to visit her, and they'd laugh together. She'd say, "Oh Chaz, you're such a romantic. Kiss me."

And he would.

February 11

"I don't think I'm going to be flying to Baltimore," Chaz announced glumly, as he dropped down on a bench beside Brian in the crowded cafeteria.

Three girls sat on the other side of the table, and Chaz felt them watching him. They were whispering and eating slowly, as if listening to his conversation with Brian.

"The man finally came to his senses," Brian mumbled around a mouthful of pizza.

Chaz glared at him. "I didn't say I wasn't going. All I meant was I won't take an airplane. Wendy misses *me* as much as I miss *her*. She said so in her last letter—"

"Which was over a week ago?"

"So?"

"What's she been doing since then, Chaz? It's not like she couldn't pick up a phone or a pen."

Chaz didn't know why he felt he had to defend Wendy. "You have no idea what she's going through," he snapped. "How would you feel if your parents dragged you halfway across the country, away from everyone and everything you'd ever known?"

He pushed himself up from the table and walked away, weaving angrily around students who jammed the spaces between tables. He felt someone following him and spun around. "Leave me alone!" he blurted out before he realized it wasn't Brian.

Rosie Samson stood blinking up at him. "I-I'm sorry, Chaz."

He groaned and rolled his eyes. "I didn't mean you, Rosie. I thought you were Brian."

She nodded. "I know you're upset, I couldn't help overhearing." Two of her friends stood behind her, looking nervous. He recognized them as the girls from the table. They, along with a bunch of other junior and senior girls, often showed up at Blue Fusion's gigs.

"Listen," Rosie said, her voice so quiet he could barely hear her over the noise in the cafeteria, "I'm having a party tomorrow night. Why don't you come over and hang with us?"

Chaz smiled sadly. "I don't think so."

"You're going to try to see Wendy, aren't you?" Rosie asked.

"Yeah. The question is, how am I going to get there? I don't have enough money to fly, and train fare is almost as high."

"That leaves the bus," Rosie said thoughtfully. "If it were up to me, I think I'd wait until I could afford to fly. Buses can be pretty grungy."

"The bus," Chaz murmured thoughtfully. He'd considered it before, then quickly dismissed it. The drive would take nearly a whole day each way, and wouldn't leave him much time to spend with Wendy.

"I took a bus to Milwaukee to visit my sister," one of the girls said. "It was scary." She shivered, remembering.

"The bus," Chaz repeated, studying the toes of his Reeboks. He'd called about the rates. He seemed to remember the round-trip fare was less than $150. If he earned just another thirty, he might be able to make it. He looked up at Rosie. "Are you planning on having live music at your party?"

Rosie's mouth dropped open. "Chaz, I can't afford to hire a band."

"You wouldn't need a whole band. I could just bring my keyboard. I used to play solo gigs a lot."

"That'd be so-o-o-o cool," one of Rosie's friends whispered. "Trish, don't you think that'd be cool?"

The third girl smiled dreamily at Chaz. "If it were my party, I'd hire you, Chaz."

Rosie scowled at her two friends, then turned back to Chaz. "How much would you charge to play for a couple of hours?"

"Fifty," he said.

"That's too much."

"Forty-five."

"I won't have that much money left after I pay for soda and chips. What about thirty?"

"Done," he said, slapping her a low five. "Baltimore, here I come."

February 12

Chaz felt as if he worked twice as hard for the thirty dollars he earned playing at Rosie's party, as he would have for the fifty or more he got on a regular job. Dragging his heavy keyboard, microphone, and the three-foot-tall amp down the narrow steps to her basement left him gasping for air.

As soon as he'd hooked up all of his equipment and run a sound test, Rosie's father appeared at the top of the stairs, yelling for him to turn down the volume. Guests started arriving, so he began playing softly. Everyone complained that the music was too quiet, so he cranked up the volume again. Mr. Samson opened the basement door and shouted at him again, so he had to turn off the amp and use only the small speakers built into the Kawai. The music sounded terrible—like wimpy cocktail lounge tunes, or the junk you hear in elevators.

By 2:00 AM, Chaz had been singing and playing for almost four hours, just to make sure Rosie knew she was getting her money's worth. She paid him his thirty, and he packed up his equipment and left.

February 13

Chaz drove home with a hoarse throat, a headache, and a cramp in his right hand. But he had another thirty bucks in his pocket, and a plan. He caught three hours' sleep, then threw a change of underwear, socks, a clean shirt and the card and heart-shaped box of candy he'd bought for Wendy into his gym bag. It was 6:30 AM.

His parents weren't thrilled when he woke them up by running the shower.

"Where are you off to this early?" his father asked as he staggered into the kitchen in his bathrobe a few minutes later.

"I told you weeks ago, Dad." Chaz poured his

father a cup of coffee and slid it across the table at him. "I'm going to Baltimore to visit Wendy."

His father rubbed both of his palms over his face and yawned. "Thought you'd given up on that idea. Lack of funds."

"I don't have enough to fly, but I called Trailways last night, and it's only $141 round trip. I can leave on a bus in an hour and get back here by ten o'clock tomorrow night, if I have to be back for school on Monday." He looked at his mother, who scuffed across the tiles in her slippers and started pulling things out of the fridge. She didn't respond to his hint that he wanted to cut school on Monday.

"You definitely have to be back," his father said in a serious tone, then he laughed and shook his head. "How much time will that give you two love birds together? An hour or two?"

Despite his father's teasing, Chaz could feel himself growing excited. What did time matter? He and Wendy would make the most of every minute, every second! "I'll arrive in Baltimore tonight at seven o'clock. I can take Wendy out for dinner or a movie, or we can just hang out at her house. I'll leave Sunday morning at ten. At least we'll be able to see each other on Valentine's Day. I want to surprise her, make it really special for her."

"This makes no sense at all," his father commented.

Chaz's mother set a package of English muffins on the counter top. "Falling in love rarely makes sense," she murmured. "It just happens."

Chaz smiled. In her own subtle way, she was telling his dad to ease up and let him go. Chaz turned back to his father, who was frowning into his coffee cup.

"Well, you're seventeen years old, and it's not as if you haven't traveled on your own before. If you've got the money . . ." He shrugged and took a gulp of his coffee. "Better take a sandwich with you for the road."

The bus depot smelled like any public place Chaz had ever known—a mix of stale food, body odor, and something gross . . . probably urine. He hadn't expected anything fancy, so he wasn't exactly disappointed. But he didn't dare let go of his travel bag even for a second, fearing someone would grab it and run.

He bought his ticket and stood by the door, not wanting to sit on any of the benches that looked sticky with suspicious substances he couldn't (and didn't want to) identify. A guy in an expensive-looking leather jacket asked him for a light, then whispered confidentially, "Wanna buy some good stuff?"

Chaz didn't have to ask what the man meant by *stuff;* he moved to the other side of the waiting room and watched as the drug pusher approached other travelers. The man appeared to make a sale on his fourth try. Chaz looked around for a security guard or cop, and wondered if it would be the same at every stop—desperate people lurking in grim waiting rooms, trying to make a hit or steal something. He'd have to stay alert the whole trip.

When a voice over the PA system finally announced that the bus for Baltimore was ready to be boarded at gate 5, Chaz rushed for the door so that he could choose a good seat, up front near the driver. But he discovered that an experienced flock of passengers had been waiting outside, and there was nothing left for him but an aisle seat near the rear of the bus. He sat beside an old woman who looked as if she hadn't slept in a week. She narrowed her eyes at him suspiciously as he wedged himself into the seat, trying not to brush up against her. Across the aisle was a man who smelled like mothballs, unbathed skin, and cigarette smoke. He was cracking open peanuts, letting the shells drop on the floor. No one talked. No one laughed. It felt as if it was going to be a very long trip.

Chaz blinked himself awake and found himself looking at a timetable. The old woman held it in trembling hands as the bus pulled out of a gas station just after they'd crossed the state border into Ohio. Noticing that she'd crossed something out and written in new figures, he leaned forward and squinted.

She turned and scowled at him. "What's your problem, young man?"

"I-I was just wondering why you'd marked out our arrival time in Baltimore."

"It's a misprint," she said sharply.

"What?"

She jabbed a wrinkled finger at the table. "They've got the wrong time here."

"They do?" Chaz's heart raced. He sat up straight in his seat. "How do you know?"

"The ticket salesman told me."

Chaz rubbed his burning eyes. "No one told *me*. What time do we arrive in Baltimore?"

"Nine-oh-five," she said. "Not that it matters on a long trip like this. A couple of hours one way or another—"

"A couple of hours!" Chaz groaned. He had so

few to spend with Wendy, and every extra second on the bus seemed like a nightmarish eternity.

He pressed himself back into the cracked vinyl seat and thought. By nine on a Saturday night, Wendy might be out with her new friends. She might even spend the night at another girl's house, although she wasn't likely to have any really close friends yet. Still, what would he do if he got there and she was out? She'd be just as disappointed as he would if they missed each other.

He smiled tiredly. Man, she was going to be so thrilled to see him. He could see her sunny grin, her eyes sparkling as brightly as the little blue topaz in the ring he'd given her for her birthday. No, he couldn't give up the idea of surprising Wendy. But he'd have to find a way to make sure she stayed home.

At the next stop he hunted up a pay phone and used the calling card his father had given him for Christmas. The idea had been to give him a way to reach home if the band got stuck on the road while traveling to or from a long-distance gig. But Chaz figured all emergencies were pretty much alike. And this was definitely an emergency.

Mrs. Rensler answered on the third ring. "Why, Chaz, a middle-of-the-day call. What a surprise!"

"Is Wendy there?" he asked quickly.

"Why yes, she is . . ." She seemed to hesitate.

"Can I talk with her?"

"Sure. Sure, Chaz. I think she's getting ready to head on over to the mall, but I know she'll want to talk to you."

Chaz kept one eye on the bus. On previous stops, the driver hadn't seemed to take notice of who got off and who came back on. Chaz didn't want to get left behind but he couldn't help feeling excited. Any minute now, Wendy would come on the line. He'd actually hear her voice.

He smiled, tapping out a rhythm from one of Blue Fusion's songs on the side of the pay phone with the edge of the card. At last he heard muffled voices—Wendy and her mom, he guessed—and then someone picked up the phone.

"Hello, Chaz." His heart soared. Chaz hadn't heard Wendy speak in over a month. He'd forgotten how strongly the sound of her words pulled at his insides.

"Hey there, beautiful, how's it going?" he asked.

"Fine," she said. "I was just on my way out."

"Yeah, your mom said. Listen—" He could hardly contain himself. He felt like blurting out his whole plan, but that would ruin the fun. "I don't want to hold you up now. I just need to make sure you'll be home tonight."

"Tonight?" She sounded puzzled.

"Yeah, there's a surprise coming for you." He chuckled to himself.

"Chaz, if you're planning on sending flowers or something, you really shouldn't. They're expensive and now that you and I—"

Just then, Chaz spotted the driver heading back toward the bus. "Gotta go!" he broke into her sentence. "Just promise me you'll be home tonight after nine o'clock."

"Chaz, I—"

"Promise me!" he shouted into the receiver. The driver was climbing the steps.

"Okay, I promise but—"

"Love ya! Gotta go!" He dropped the receiver into the metal cradle and ran for the bus.

The engine was already revving up when he hit the first step. As Chaz passed the driver, the man shot him an impatient look.

The old lady cracked open one eye when Chaz dropped into his seat, breathing hard. "He was going to leave without you," she muttered. "I told him to wait or I'd complain to the bus company."

"Thanks," Chaz said.

"You should buy me a sandwich at the next stop," she stated. "And a cup of coffee."

"Okay," he agreed, although if he did he wouldn't be able to afford anything for himself.

He rested his head back on the plastic cushion and wondered how many hours had passed since he'd eaten the sandwich and apple he'd brought from home. His stomach growled. Trying to ignore it, he recalled the cool, silky sound of Wendy's voice. He thought about her long fingers combing lightly through the short hairs on the back of his neck when he would, at last, hold her and they'd kiss.

Tonight was going to be great!

The Trailways bus pulled into the Baltimore Transit Depot at 9:05 PM. Chaz jumped off, a quarter in his hand, racing for the pay phones. He punched in Wendy's number but hung up on the first ring, before she could answer. Which was better? Calling to be sure she was there? Or just showing up?

She'd promised she would be home. He turned away from the phone after fishing his quarter out of the coin return, and smiled. Of course she'd be waiting for him—probably expecting another phone call or a delivery for Valentine's Day. He bet she had no idea what his surprise was! He couldn't wait to see her face when she opened her front door to find him standing there.

He envisioned her blond hair brushed in glistening strands away from her face. Her blue eyes sparkling, her mouth wide with surprise. She'd stare at him in disbelief for several seconds, before rushing into his arms. He could almost feel her trembling, crying from happiness at seeing him again.

Chaz strode out into the wide lobby. The depot was a lot cleaner and less scary than the other stops had been. A kiosk with brightly colored signs was selling bagels, muffins, coffee. A tired-looking man was chasing two little boys across the waiting area. A group of teenagers was sitting on the floor in the corner; two were lying down, using knapsacks for pillows. Another bus was loading up outside, but it must not have been the one the kids were taking because they weren't paying any attention to it.

The smell of the coffee and pastries made Chaz's stomach growl with hunger. He checked his wallet. After buying the sandwich for the old lady on the bus, all he had left was a twenty-dollar bill. He wasn't sure how much the cab fare would be to Wendy's house, so he didn't dare spend any of it on food. Besides, Wendy would probably want to make him something to eat at her house. Her mom always had a couple of pizzas in the freezer and a supply of lunch meats. He imagined two thick slices of rye bread, slathered with mustard and stacked with layers of ham and Swiss cheese, lettuce and tomatoes.

Feeling a sudden surge of energy at the thought of Wendy's warm arms and some food in his stomach, Chaz pushed through the sooty glass doors and looked around outside. A line of cabs was parked on his left and he waved at the first driver.

"Can you take me here?" Chaz asked, holding the slip of paper on which he'd written Wendy's address up to the passenger window.

The driver rolled down the window, took the paper from him and studied it for a minute before observing Chaz through narrowed eyes. "You got cash on you, boy?"

"Right here." Chaz waved the twenty.

"That'll about do it."

Chaz hesitated. "You mean, round trip. Right?"

The man scowled at him. "Why you going all the way out to Reisterstown Road if you're just going to turn around and come back?"

"Well, I'm not . . . not really," Chaz stammered. "I mean, I'll be there for the night, then come back here early in the morning."

"And you expected me to cool my heels and wait for you?" The driver chewed something dark and juicy that smelled awful.

"No. I thought I'd just call in the morning for another ride. I figured ten bucks each way . . . maybe?" Chaz looked at the man hopefully, then down at the lonely bill in his hand—the last of his money.

He didn't have much choice. He'd have to pay the going rate, even if it used up every cent he had. Besides, Wendy must still have her little Honda. She could drive him back to the bus depot in the morning. "Let's go," Chaz said.

The cab stopped in front of a brick townhouse with three cement steps climbing to a green front door. "That'll be nineteen-thirty," the driver said.

Chaz handed him the twenty. "I don't have any more. Seventy cents isn't much of a tip."

The driver nodded grimly. "Story of my life."

Chaz slid out of the cab onto the dark street, and climbed the steps to Wendy's door. He was exhausted and hungry, but he couldn't help smiling. He'd made it to her house. In another minute she'd open her door, and everything would be perfect.

He pushed the doorbell and waited, his heart throbbing in his throat. While Chaz waited, he searched through his bag and dug the heart-shaped box of chocolates from beneath his blue jeans. *I should have brought flowers too,* he thought. But he hadn't had enough money, and even if he'd had extra cash he couldn't have carried a bouquet on the bus without its wilting or getting crushed.

Chaz held the chocolates in front of him so that Wendy would see the fancy lace-and-satin lid the moment she opened the door. He waited. No one came to answer the bell.

He rang again. From inside the house, he heard a distant jingle. At last, a shadow passed across the glass panel beside the door, just before it swung open.

"Chaz, what are you doing here?" It was Wendy's mother, and a shocked frown tugged her eyebrows downward.

"Hi, Mrs. Rensler. I think Wendy is expecting me . . . or at least expecting something." He laughed out loud at the mystified expression on the woman's face. Anticipating Wendy's squeal of glee when she first saw him, he stepped forward to go inside, but Mrs. Rensler didn't move from the doorway.

She peered past him, into the dark street. "Where's your car, Chaz?"

"Took the bus." He tried to see into the house, but the hallway wasn't very well lighted. "No reason to bring a car when Wendy has hers. Where is she, anyway?"

The woman chewed on her lower lip, looking nervous. "Downstairs in the rec room, but I don't think she—"

Too excited to wait any longer for her to invite him inside, Chaz dodged around Wendy's mom, into the foyer. He spotted a door halfway down the hallway, opened it and immediately heard music—strains of Mariah Carey's new album drifting up the stairway to him. Wendy loved Mariah's music. She'd patterned her singing style after the popular vocalist. Usually, she sang along with the cuts on the CD. She wasn't singing now.

The lights were off in the basement. Chaz could hardly see the steps below his feet. He set his gym bag on the top step and wedged the red foil, heart-shaped box under his arm, squinting into the darkness. Wendy must have fallen asleep on the couch, he reasoned. He could see the tan plaid upholstery covering its back, from across the paneled rec room. Grinning, he reached for the light switch.

There was a soft moan.

Then a voice issued softly out of the dark. "Kiss me again." Wendy's voice. He recognized it for sure.

Chaz froze, only his finger moving to click on the light switch.

As soon as the overhead fluorescent bulbs flickered brightly, two heads appeared over the back of the couch. Wendy's blond hair was mussed. A boy he didn't know blinked at him.

"What the hell you doin', man?" the boy demanded.

Unable to move, Chaz stood with his mouth open, his stomach tied in knots. He desperately wanted to turn and run back up the stairs, away from the sight of Wendy in another guy's arms. But his feet felt as if they were Superglued to the steps, and his mouth refused to produce any sound at all.

He stared numbly at the couple on the couch. The couple that should have been him and Wendy.

"Chaz?" Wendy finally said, frowning at him. "What are you doing here?"

"T-tomorrow's Valentine's Day," he blurted out, and looked down at the heart full of candy still stuck between his elbow and ribs.

"You came all the way from Chicago?" She laughed. "I don't believe you. After my letter, I figured you understood. Like, you know, we're done . . . through."

"Letter?" It took him a minute to sift back through his memories. The only letter he could recall in any detail was the one Rush had half eaten. Wendy had said she missed him, that they'd always be together.

"The letter telling you I thought we should break up . . . remember?" Wendy rolled her eyes when he didn't answer her. Pushing herself up off of the couch, she smoothed out her rumpled skirt and blouse. "Chaz, come on upstairs."

"What about me?" the boy on the couch asked.

"I'll be right back, Duncan. Just chill for a minute, okay?"

Chaz glowered at the other boy, then followed Wendy up the stairs. Her mother was waiting for them in the kitchen, looking worried.

"No one hit anyone, or anything like that," Wendy grumbled. She spun around, her tangled blonde hair flying when she stopped to face Chaz. "Now, tell me what you're doing here."

He held out the box of chocolates to her. She took it and slammed it down on the table without looking at it.

"I . . . I thought you missed me," Chaz choked out. "My dog ate half of your letter, and in the part that was left you said . . ." He pulled the scrap of paper from his wallet and flattened it out on the kitchen table.

Wendy stared at it, reading slowly, her mouth silently forming the words. "Oh," she said dully, at last.

"I wanted to surprise you for Valentine's Day," Chaz said woodenly. His stomach felt as if it were a meat grinder, chewing him to pieces from the inside out.

Wendy scowled at him, her blue eyes cold, an irritated tightness pulling her lips.

Mrs. Rensler coughed and said diplomatically, "Well, I think that's very sweet, Chaz."

Suddenly, anger boiled up inside of Chaz. He thought, *I nearly killed myself getting to Baltimore and this is the thanks I get?*

Jerking himself around, he stomped out of the kitchen, down the dim hallway, and out through the front door into the night.

He ran as hard as he could for a half-dozen blocks before the angry black haze faded from before his eyes, enabling him to think again. Taking the letter out of his pocket, he stared at it in the pale orange glow of a street lamp. The missing words he'd thought were so unimportant, they'd obviously been meant to tell him good-bye.

"After all, as close as we have been, we both

know . . ." he supplied another variation on the missing words, "we can't be together for always." The rest was probably the same—a kiss-off . . . a Dear John letter. He'd been dumped, and he hadn't even known it.

Chaz tore up the letter and let the scraps drift into the gutter. Only then did he realize he hadn't remembered his gym bag. It wasn't worth going back for, he decided. Just some clothes and a card for a girl who was no longer his Valentine. His return bus ticket was in his wallet. That was all he needed. He started walking, wondering dismally how many miles it was back to the bus terminal.

February 14, Valentine's Day

It had been around 10:00 PM when Chaz left Wendy's house. By the time he reached the downtown terminal, it was almost light out. He'd walked all night through the cold. The last few miles it had rained.

He had no dry clothes to change into and no money to buy anything to wear. He went straight into the men's room and punched the hand drier and stood in front of the blast of hot air, shivering.

When Chaz finally felt a little warmer, he used the toilet, washed his face and hands, finger-combed his hair, and took a long drink of water from the faucet. He still hadn't eaten since the day before, and his stomach felt hollow and tight as a drum head.

Chaz walked back out into the lobby. Three teenagers with beat-up musical instruments—an acoustic guitar, a bongo drum, and flimsy-looking keyboard that must have been ten years old—were playing for coins passers-by tossed into their jar. He couldn't see why the kids bothered, because no one much was around.

Chaz slumped onto the nearest bench, his head in his hands, and tried to shut out the world. How could the fantastic weekend he'd planned have turned out so rotten?

The sound of music eventually broke through his black thoughts. The street band's melodies were a mix of twangy island sounds and New Orleans funk. The three young musicians were pretty good, he thought. Much better than a lot of bands with fancy electronic equipment that got gigs in Chicago.

He raised his head and listened, letting the notes lift him to his feet. Slowly he walked closer, then stood behind the keyboard player, watching the boy's hands.

"If you come down heavier with your left hand, it'll sound even better," he murmured, unaware that he was speaking out loud until the boy looked up at him.

"You play, man?"

"Yeah," he said. "I play. Ever heard of Blue Fusion?"

The boy shook his head. "Ever heard of Crusty Crew?"

"No. Who are they?"

The boy grinned. "Us."

Chaz smiled back at him.

"Want to sit in?" the guitarist asked. "Give him the board, Donny."

The keyboard player stepped to one side and waved to Chaz. Chaz nodded, took a deep breath, and rested his hands on the keys. Just the feeling of the instrument under his fingertips was soothing.

He recognized the song the guitar and drum were picking out, and he found the right key and started in, playing softly at first, then feeling more sure of himself. The music seemed to swell and fill the bus station.

After a few minutes, a gingery, slightly gravelly voice joined them.

Chaz looked up to see a girl with a travel bag slung over one shoulder, her mouth open on a long note. She had short brown hair and eyes the color of jade, so green they snapped at him. Her glance locked with his as she sang, and he played to her voice, gentling his notes so they wouldn't drown her out.

"What's your name?" he whispered.

"Jasmine," she said between phrases, then continued singing in a voice so rich it rumbled through his gut, down to his toes.

"You'd do great, singing in clubs in Chicago," he said. His hands left the keyboard, and the music stopped.

She smiled at him. "Good, that's where I'm going. Know any bands that need a singer?"

Chaz grinned as he stood up and took her hand to lead her to the nearest bench. "I know a great band you'd be perfect for." He felt giddy. "Want to be my Valentine?"

She laughed at him. "What?"

"Never mind," he said laughing along with her, because her happiness seemed contagious. He thought he'd never seen prettier eyes in his life. "We'll have to work up to that."

Kathryn Jensen

Valentine's Day meant pressure, big time, when I was a teenager. All the girls in my class compared piles of cards at the end of the day. This was a primo-serious matter. Who had gotten the most Valentines? Who was given the single most romantic and elaborate card? Did anyone get a love missive from Michael Willis, the tenth-grade Troy Donohue clone? (Author's Note: TD was the hunkiest actor in Hollywood back then. If you're reading this, Troy, I still love you!) Which unlucky girl had received a card from the class geek? The only worse fate was dragging yourself home with no Valentines at all.

Most of my girlfriends would have happily given away their favorite Beatles album to be surprised by a boy like Chaz. That never happened, but a few of us were lucky enough to find a red rose in our lockers or a red satin heart full of chocolates waiting for us at home. (If you were really lucky, it wasn't from your father!) One thing was for sure, Valentine's Day always kept us guessing.

KATHRYN JENSEN has written twenty-eight novels full of romance, suspense, and fun for adults and young readers. Her mysteries for young-adult readers are written under the pen name Nicole Davidson, which is a combination of her daughter's and son's names. (They like seeing their names on book covers.) She lives in Maryland with her sweetheart Bill, who happens to be her husband. Over the years, she has celebrated Valentine's Day in many romantic places, including Texas, Italy, and Connecticut.

Will You Be My Valentine?

Cameron Dokey

I'll only tell you this story on one condition.

That you promise never to reveal it to another living soul.

Now, I know this sounds like an unreasonable expectation. But honestly, it isn't. Not when you take into consideration the fact that I'm about to relate the most embarrassing moments of my entire life.

And it isn't that my story doesn't have a happy ending. Amazingly enough, it does. But the way I see it, the fact that things really did turn out happily ever after doesn't make a difference. Not in terms of whether or not you get to reveal what I'm about to tell you to another living soul.

Parts of this story are *extremely embarrassing.* At least, they're extremely embarrassing to me.

I've had other embarrassing moments, of course. I mean, I wouldn't want you to think the events of that fateful Valentine's Day were the only embarrassing things that ever happened to me.

There was, for instance, the time in English when Mrs. Rueter caught me writing a note to my best friend, Rene Jackson, and then she made me read the note out loud. It was all about how my boyfriend and I had been practicing French kissing. I have to say that was pretty embarrassing.

And then there was the time we were supposed to run the fifty-yard dash in PE only I forgot to wear a bra.

But I think I have to say, with the exception of my Valentine's story, that the incident in the library with the IEFO was really the most embarrassing thing that ever happened to me. Actually, the IEFO incident sort of leads into the Valentine incident. So, as long as I've committed myself to revealing the most embarrassing moments of my life, I guess I may as well start with the IEFO.

You know about IEFOs, of course. Incredibly Embarrassing Flying Objects. Well, I had a close encounter all my own. What happened was, I reached into my very cluttered purse to pull out a pen during library study. But when I yanked the pen out, I accidentally hurled this tampon all the way across the room.

Now, I know things are supposed to be quiet in a library. I mean, people are always saying how silent libraries are. That's part of the whole purpose of them, right? *Quiet study.* But this library, on this occasion, gave a whole new meaning to the term.

You could have done more than heard a pin drop in that library. You could have heard the blood rushing through my classmates' veins. You could have heard their eyeballs bulging out of their eye sockets. And you certainly could have heard their neck muscles creaking as they craned their heads forward, staring in amazement at the sight of the IEFO.

Don't tell me it's not possible to hear things like that. I heard them, so I ought to know. Though I still haven't figured out what all the girls were staring at. I mean, it's not as if they hadn't seen one of those objects before.

Naturally, I wasn't coherent enough to think of any of this at the time. Not a chance. No way. I was far too busy wishing I was someplace else. Anyplace else. But preferably someplace that didn't have any people in it.

And that includes John Mulholland.

The tampon ended up next to him.

Well, not *next* to him, exactly. I guess I'd have to say *in front* of him. In his history book, to be exact. Right in the middle of it, as the book sat open on the library table. I think we were studying the Spanish Inquisition at the time.

I remember because suddenly I realized that I had something in common with all those people tortured by the Spanish Inquisition. I was sure I knew exactly how they felt. I hadn't done anything wrong. But I knew beyond a shadow of a doubt what was going to happen next.

I was absolutely certain I was going to die.

I still remember the way John stared down at his history textbook. I remember how he lifted his head and looked around. I've never been quite sure how he knew that I was the owner of the IEFO. I mean, it didn't have my name engraved on it or anything. I guess it was because when I saw him looking over at me, my courage finally gave out. I groaned and put my head down in my arms.

John Mulholland is one of the biggest hunks at school. Every girl I know has been in love with him for years. Like all the rest, I'd always wondered what I'd have to do to get his attention. But in my wildest nightmare, I never could have come up with this plan.

John's chair scraped against the floor as he pushed back from the table. I heard a soft, scratching sound as he picked up his history book. His shoes squeaked just a little as he walked slowly across the library.

The squeaking slowed down as he neared my table, then stopped altogether.

"Excuse me," a voice somewhere above my right ear said. I'll say this for him: John Mulholland has a very nice voice. It's warm and rich and smooth, sort of like the chocolate sauce on a hot fudge sundae.

I listened, but I couldn't hear the slightest hint of laughter in his voice.

In the end, I think that was the only thing that enabled me to lift my head up. The fact that it didn't sound like John was laughing at me.

I stared at him, the library around us still unnaturally silent. He held his history book out toward me. The flying tampon was still nestled amid its open pages.

"Pardon me for asking, but does this incredibly amazing flying object belong to you?"

"Incredibly embarrassing," I corrected.

John's brow wrinkled. He looked at me as if I was speaking in a foreign tongue. "Incredibly what?" he asked.

"Incredibly *embarrassing,"* I repeated, emphasizing the second word just a little. "Incredibly *embarrassing* flying object. I-*E*-F-O. I'd have to say that you've done more than just made a sighting here, Mr. Mulholland. I'd have to say that you've made actual contact. You could be famous. I hope you realize that. Why, I'll bet Agents Mulder and Scully will soon be knocking on your door."

Oh my God, I thought. *I'm babbling.* But what else was I supposed to do? I mean, I ask you. It's not like I'd had any training in this sort of situation. This had definitely not been covered in *The Seventeen Book of Etiquette and Young Living* my grandmother had given me for my sixteenth birthday.

"Hmm, well," John finally answered. His eyes stared down at the IEFO. Then they lifted to stare at me.

I probably don't have to tell you that John's eyes are gorgeous. This totally amazing shade of blue-green. With a shock, I noticed that they were kind of sparkling as he looked down at me. Then the sparkle turned into a shine. Before I realized what was happening, John Mulholland's amazing eyes were laughing.

Not *at* me, but *with* me.

"Yes, well, Ms. Reeves, I think I see your point. About this being an Incredibly *Embarrassing* Flying Object, I mean. But I don't think there's any need to involve the FBI at this point. Let's just keep this between ourselves, shall we?"

John leaned over and tilted his history textbook. The IEFO slid off of his book onto mine. I slammed my book shut and stuffed both it and the IEFO into my backpack. Just at that moment, the school bell rang.

The rest of my classmates stampeded for the library exit. Being very, and I do mean *very,* careful not to look at me. But John Mulholland didn't move a muscle. He continued to stand there, his eyes smiling.

And that's when it happened. That's the moment I fell in love with him.

Now, I don't want you to think that all this was too sudden. I mean, it's not every day I do this kind of thing. And certainly not in such incredibly embarrassing circumstances. But there was something about the way John handled the whole situation that just reached right out and grabbed me.

Other guys would have stuck their fingers down

their throats and gagged at the sight of that Incredibly Embarrassing Flying Object. Other guys would have handled their embarrassment by trying to embarrass me. But John simply returned my IEFO to me, being careful not to touch it, of course. There was no sense in getting too personal, after all.

"So, Jessie," he said, as he helped me gather my belongings and finally escape the library.

I can't believe it, I thought. *He knows my name.*

"Do you have to get home right away or anything?" Library study was always last period.

"No," I said, only trusting my voice with words of one syllable.

John's eyes were still smiling. "I don't suppose I could interest you in an Italian soda," he said.

Before I could stop myself I answered, "It depends on what kind."

Now, my best friend, Rene, would have been appalled at this answer. She says my smart mouth gets me into trouble all the time. But John actually thought that my remark was funny. He laughed at it, anyway. Even his laughter was wonderful. It washed over me like clear morning light.

"Whatever kind you want," he answered.

"Okay," I said. "You're on."

And that was the beginning of how everything happened. The most embarrassing events of my entire life, that is. Though, at that moment, there wasn't a cloud on my horizon. Not after the IEFO got safely tucked away.

John and I went to Besto Espresso. As far as I was concerned, it was the coolest espresso bar in town. Instead of uncomfortable stools and rickety little bistro tables, it had these great big comfy chairs. The walls had been painted to look like an old Italian villa. And all these black-and-white photos of Italian cities adorned the walls.

But the best thing was, Besto Espresso had a fireplace. They kept it going all the time. Well, not when it got really hot in the summer, of course. But definitely in February when it can still get cold. And believe it or not, when John and I walked in, the seats in front of the fireplace were empty.

"Hey, Jessie, why don't you go snag those chairs," John said as we came through the doorway. He gave me a little scoot with a hand in the middle of my back. All of a sudden, my whole body felt warm.

"I'll go get our sodas," he continued. "What kind do you want?"

"Mandarine," I said, hoping to impress him just a little. Actually, of course, it was just an orange soda.

"Okay," John answered. "You got it. One Mandarine Italian Soda coming right up. You want the works, right? Whipped cream and everything?"

"I want it all," I answered, then blushed like an idiot. But John just smiled. He went to stand in line, while I saved the seats in front of the fire. While he got our sodas, I tried to convince myself that it was sitting near the fire that had made my face so warm.

Eventually, he came back holding two huge Italian sodas. Ribbons of whipped cream adorned their tops. Ice cubes rattled softly against the sides of their clear plastic glasses. Mine was this beautiful, pale orange color. Just like orange sherbet. John's Italian soda was a color I'd never seen before. A green so bright I thought for sure it would glow in the dark.

"What kind is it?" I said, eyeing it a little doubtfully as he set it down on the table. He chuckled as he settled into the comfy chair.

"I don't know. I liked the color so I ordered it."

"A man who's bold and daring," I said. "I like that." Another remark that would have sent Rene running for cover. *What's come over me this afternoon?* I wondered.

"Do you?" John said, chewing on his straw. His eyes watched me, slightly speculative. "So, Jessie, don't you hang out with the drama club a lot?"

A quick chill swept over me, in spite of the fire. "Yeah," I answered, my senses going on full alert.

Not everyone at school likes drama club members. Some people think we're weird or something. And some people think that girls who are into drama like to party hearty. I wondered if that was the reason for John's sudden interest. Feeling slightly sick, I took a sip of soda.

"I've been thinking of maybe trying out for a play."

I choked, sending little gobs of whipped cream flying. "You are?" I managed to get out, fumbling for my napkin. "That's great, John."

I felt so relieved, I could hardly believe it. In my mind's eye, I could see the way things would be. John would become a member of the drama club. Mr. Barnes was casting the next show in just a few weeks. Naturally, John would play the lead. Also naturally, I would play opposite him. He'd discover how incredibly talented I was and we'd fall madly in love.

"So, do you, like, have any pointers or anything?" he continued.

"About what?" I murmured, wiping whipped cream off the table, my mind still busy with the details of our love life.

"About trying out for a play."

"Oh, that," I said, feeling my face start to heat up.

If I didn't start paying attention we'd never get to the part where he discovered how enormously talented I was. We'd stop right here, with him writing me off as an IEFO-flinging moron.

"Well, I think the best thing is to just be yourself," I said. "I mean, I know that sounds kind of dorky, but Mr. Barnes isn't into a lot of phony stuff. No weird accents or rubber noses. He just wants to know that you can make sense of what the character has to say. And it's important that you listen to your scene partner. He's really into that. He says that's why the playwrights call it dialogue."

John's eyes lit up and he gave a warm chuckle. "That's pretty good," he said. "I think I just might like this guy. So, tryouts are pretty soon, right?"

"Auditions," I corrected.

"What?"

"We don't call them tryouts. We call them auditions. And they're the Monday after Valentine's Day. That gives you all weekend to rest up from the Snuggle Bunny Sock Hop." I don't know who came up with the name for that particular event, but whoever it is ought to have their brain drained.

"Oh, yeah," John said, his tone thoughtful. All of a sudden, this really strange expression came over his face. He looked kind of embarrassed. Like I'd caught him doing something he wasn't supposed to. "The dance," he said.

I could feel my whole body start to pound with embarrassment. *Well, Jessie, you certainly put your foot right in that one,* I thought. From the look on his face, I guessed I'd brought up the last subject in the world John wanted to talk about.

The Snuggle Bunny Sock Hop, a.k.a. the Valentine's Day Dance.

Our school has this incredibly weird tradition. The Valentine's Day Dance is girl ask guy.

Now, I ask you. Have you ever heard of anything so disgusting? I don't think I've ever encountered anything so unfair. I mean, it's not like things aren't hard enough for a girl on Valentine's Day. If you've got a Valentine, I guess it's terrific. But if you haven't, let's face it, it's pretty depressing.

So what did the school authorities decide to do? They decided to go and pile on all this added pressure. Now if a girl doesn't go to the Valentine's dance it's all *her* fault. Personally, I think it's a male chauvinist plot to get back at liberated females.

And now I'd gone and mentioned the unmentionable. I'd actually said the words *Snuggle Bunny Sock Hop.* I'd said them out loud. And I hadn't done it in the privacy of my own bedroom, where I might be safe. Oh, no. I'd done it sitting across from one of the biggest hunks in the entire school. Girls probably lined up outside his door to ask him out. The tears shed over a John Mulholland rejection could probably fill a swimming pool.

Right this moment, I was sure he was starting to panic. Sure he was thinking I'd brought the subject up deliberately, so I could blindside him and ask him to the dance. Maybe he was even thinking I'd tossed that IEFO at him on purpose. It had certainly gotten his attention, hadn't it?"

Please, I thought, *let me find a way out of this. I'll never let my mouth get carried away again.* Valentine's Day was in just two weeks. Between now and then, it was peak Valentine's Dance date-hunting season. And let's face it, John Mulholland was prime prey. Right about now, he was probably starting to feel like an endangered species. That probably explained the weird look on his face.

So I did the only thing that I could think of. I decided to let him get away. There was no reason for him to panic. Not when I could do it so much better.

"Oh, my goodness!" I shrieked, sounding exactly like my grandmother when she's discovered a large insect. "Will you look at the time? I've got to get home. I didn't know it was so late. Thank you for the soda. It was really lovely, John." Before he could get a word in edgewise, I grabbed my backpack and bolted.

"Jessie," John called out, just before I made it to the door. Slowly, heart thundering, I turned around. He still sat in front of the fire, his cup of bright green soda glowing on the table. Moisture beaded and ran like tears down the sides.

"See you around?" John said, his voice kind of quiet.

My heart gave a painful lurch. "Yeah, okay," I answered. "Sure. Tryouts, maybe. Don't forget."

"Auditions," he corrected, with a slow smile. "Don't worry. I won't forget. They're the Monday after Valentine's Day."

There was something about the way he said it. Something about the tone of his voice when he said the words *Valentine's Day.* All of a sudden I felt like a fool for running. Felt like I was throwing something wonderful away.

But I was never going to know now. I'd hit the panic button and it was too late to turn back now. I walked home, wondering if I'd just missed the most perfect opportunity of my life.

As soon as I got home, I called Rene.

Rene Jackson and I have been best friends forever. Ever since we discovered that our initials were complementary. I'm JR. And she's RJ. Not only that, our looks are complementary. I'm short and brown-haired. She's a tall blonde.

Rene and I confide everything to each other. There are absolutely no secrets between us. So, naturally I had to tell her how badly I'd just blown things with John Mulholland. And naturally, I had to tell her that I thought it was the biggest tragedy of my entire life. Particularly since, on the way home, I'd decided he was probably my one and only true love.

"I just don't understand why it has to be so hard!" I said, as we lay flopped across my bed later that evening. We'd polished off our homework, and were drowning our sorrows in big dishes of Rainforest Crunch ice cream. If you're going to consume mega-calories, the least you can do is consume them for a worthy cause.

"I mean, when *I* thought that *he* thought I was about to ask him to the Snuggle Bunny Sock Hop, I totally panicked. I swear, I could literally feel ice cubes flowing through my veins. It just can't be this hard to ask a guy out. Not for other people."

Rene licked the ice cream off her spoon reflectively. "Oh, I don't know," she said. "It is for me."

That made me sit straight up, I can tell you. The fact that Rene wanted to ask someone to the Snuggle Bunny Sock Hop was news to me. She hadn't dropped so much as a hint.

"Okay, spill it," I said. "Who is he?"

Rene's eyes slid over to my dresser. *Uh oh,* I thought. *She's avoiding something.*

"You're never going to believe it," she finally spoke up.

My eyes narrowed. "Try me." Was she going to tell me *she* wanted to ask John out? *"Before* you eat that enormous bite of ice cream." I know a stalling technique when I see one.

Rene left her spoon suspended in midair. "Stan Morris," she said softly.

I dropped my ice-cream spoon into my bowl with a clatter. "Stan Morris," I shouted. "My close personal friend? President of the junior class? That Stan Morris?"

Rene nodded, her eyes on her rapidly melting Rainforest Crunch as it sat in its spoon.

"You're kidding."

Rene's eyes jerked to my face. I could tell by their expression that I'd really hurt her. "I am not kidding," she said, her voice wavering just a little. "I've loved him forever. Why shouldn't I ask him?"

"I'm not saying you shouldn't," I said, my tone soothing. I really hadn't meant to upset her. "It's just—I guess I'm still getting used to the idea. Wow," I went on, shaking my head. "Stan Morris."

"May I please eat my ice cream?"

I nodded, and Rene put the spoon in her mouth. She chewed and swallowed while I considered things.

It's kind of hard to describe Stan Morris. I can't really think of anybody else at school who's quite like him. For one thing, he does just about everything. Except major sports I guess. Though he could be a basketball player because he's really tall. He's got blonde hair and blue eyes, just like Rene does, in fact.

But the thing that's always interested Stan the most is student government. For reasons that are totally beyond me, he thinks it's fascinating. He's been on the student council since we were freshmen. He's president of the junior class this year. He's also in the drama club with us. And he's on the debate team. But I think the most amazing thing about Stan Morris is the way he gets along with people. Absolutely everybody likes him.

Stan and I sort of grew up together. In fact, for a while he used to live next door to me. We've been really good friends for as long as I can remember. So I've never really considered him as potential date material. Even so, I was pretty blown away at the thought of Rene asking Stan out. I mean, I just wasn't sure how I felt about it.

Well, why not? I thought, as I polished off the last of my Rainforest Crunch. Rene was my best girlfriend. Stan was my best guy friend. Why shouldn't they find happiness together?

"Well, I think it's fabulous," I said, setting my empty ice cream dish on my dresser. "I think you should go for it, Rene."

Rene's eyes widened. "You think so?" she said. "You honestly do? Oh, Jessie, I'm so glad to hear you say that. I was afraid that you'd be mad or something. I mean, I know the two of you are really close."

"Well, yeah," I said. "But that doesn't mean I want to go out with him."

"I don't see why not. He's absolutely gorgeous."

"Rene," I said. "I can't fall in love with the boy next door. It's way too hokey."

"Well, yeah," Rene agreed instantly. "But he's not the boy next door anymore."

Now I have to say that I was really struck by this. It was true, of course. It had been years since Stan and I had actually lived next door. But I still thought of him that way, and I guess that was the thing that really mattered.

"You really think I should do it?" Rene broke into my thoughts. "You really think I should ask him out?" Sometimes, Rene needs a lot of encouragement. She's a little tentative at times. So I nodded my head emphatically to show my absolute approval.

"Of course I think you should do it. In fact, I think you shouldn't waste any time. Stan's really popular. All kinds of other girls are going to want to be his Valentine. If you want to take him to the Snuggle Bunny Sock Hop, you're going to have to jump in ahead of the crowd."

Rene made a face at my bad pun. But I could tell she was thinking things over. I could almost see her telling herself she had to be brave. "Okay," she said. "I'll do it. By the end of school tomorrow. I'll call you tomorrow night and let you know how it goes."

I leaned over and gave her a quick hug. "I wish I could be there to see the look on his face," I said. "This is going to be out of this world."

In the embarrassing and depressing days to come, I remembered this moment. Remembered the fact that I'd encouraged her to go out with him. But at the time, it didn't seem particularly significant. It just seemed like something a best friend would do.

Rene and I talked about guys for a little while longer. Then she went home and I watched some TV. I went to bed and had dreams full of hearts and flowers. Rene and I both found true love in my dreams. When I woke up in the morning, the sun was shining. The whole world looked rosy. But on the way to school, something funny happened. All of a sudden, things didn't seem so rosy for me.

Rene had her true love all picked out. And I suppose the truth was that I did, too. But I'd already blown my big chance, whereas Rene's was still coming up. She still had something to look forward to. The only thing I had to look forward to was the anguish of hearing about how John was going to go to the Valentine's Day Dance with some other girl. *I* was the one who wanted to be his number one Snuggle Bunny. Whatever that was.

By the time I got to school, I was totally depressed. My big mouth had blown it again. The day seemed to drag on forever. The only good thing about it was that most of the time I was so miserable, I was totally oblivious to my surroundings.

I do know that at some point, John came and sat next to me in one of the classes we had together. But I was so confused and freaked out I could hardly bring myself to look at him. And coherent conversation was completely out of the question. How could I just come out and say I was sorry about the way I'd run off yesterday? And I could hardly admit I'd fallen head-over-heels in love with him.

So I moped through the day, telling myself I didn't notice the puzzled, slightly hurt look in John's eyes every time he looked over at me. Telling myself it didn't matter anyway. We could never have been meant to be together. But no matter how often I told myself, never once did I believe it.

"Jessie, honey, are you all right?" My mother's voice slowly filtered through my consciousness. *Hey,* I thought. *What's my mom doing at school?* I looked over at her, wondering if maybe all of this was just a bad dream. I'd wake up and John and I would still be at Besto Espresso.

"Jessie?" my mom's voice said again. With a start, I realized I was sitting at the kitchen table. School had gotten out hours ago. I had no idea what had happened to my last few periods. No idea how I'd gotten home. It was as if I'd fallen asleep and awakened hours later to find myself at the dinner table.

From the smell, I could tell we were having my little brother's favorite: hot dogs and beans. And sauerkraut, which my father loves but which I hate, loathe, and detest.

"Sure, I'm all right, Mom." I picked up my fork, to show everything was normal. "What makes you ask?" My little brother, Billy, made a sound between a snicker and a snort.

"Check out your plate, lame brain."

"William," my mother murmured in reproof. I stared down at my dinner plate. I didn't see any hot dogs. I didn't see any beans. All I saw was this enormous pile of sauerkraut. Like, an entire lifetime's worth.

"Ahhh!" I screamed, dropping my fork and pushing the plate away as fast as I could. "Who gave all that sauerkraut to me?"

My father spoke up for the first time that evening. "You put it there, Jessie. I asked you to pass me the sauerkraut, you picked up the serving dish, and emptied the entire contents onto your plate."

I stared at the steaming pile of sauerkraut. It looked like something from another planet. Like alien intestines, maybe. Or alien brains. I had absolutely no memory of the actions my father had just mentioned. Maybe I was so upset over losing John Mulholland I'd started having blackouts.

"I did? Are you sure about that, Dad?"

My father nodded, his face solemn. I heard my mother make a worried sound.

"Trade you," I said, picking up my plate and thrusting it toward my father. He took it without a word. "I don't feel very good," I said, as soon as he'd removed the saukerkraut to a minimum safe distance. "May I please be excused?"

"But you haven't had any dinner," my mother protested.

"I'll eat later," I said, pushing back from the table. Before my mom could come up with another argument, I tossed my napkin on my chair and dashed upstairs. Safely in my room, I threw myself across my bed.

I have totally lost it, I thought. *And this has broken all previous records as the world's most horrible day.*

No sooner had I thought this than the phone beside my bed rang. My parents did this really cool thing for my last birthday. They let me have a phone in my room. I even have my own phone number, so other people in the household get a chance to talk sometimes.

"Hello?" I said, not really caring who might be calling. For all I knew, it was some carpet salesman.

"Hey, Jessie," a warm voice sounded. All of a sudden, I sat straight up. It was the one person in the world who always made me feel better.

"Stan?"

"The one and only," Stan Morris answered. "So, how's it going?"

I slumped back against the bedspread, cradling

the phone between my ear and the bed. All the events of yesterday and today came rushing back in horrifying detail. "You really don't want me to answer that question."

I heard Stan's warm chuckle dance along the phone lines. "I don't, huh?"

"You don't," I repeated. "Not now, not ever. Just trust me on this one, Stan."

"Well, I thought something might be up," Stan commented, still cheerful. "You did seem a little, well, out of it at school today."

Out of it, I thought. *Now there was an understatement.* "Gee, thanks for noticing," I said sarcastically.

"Don't mention it," Stan said, totally unflappable. "After all, what are friends for?" There was a tiny silence. I could hear him breathing into the phone. "So," he finally continued. "Are you going to tell your Uncle Stanley what's the matter? Or do I have to come over there and put the thumbscrews on?"

That made me laugh. I couldn't help it. It's part of the reason I really like Stan. He's not afraid to say really off-the-wall stuff. "Oh, no," I cried, laughter still in my voice. "Not the thumbscrews."

"You're a wimp, Reeves. You know that, don't you?"

"Yeah, well," I answered. "It takes one to know one." My little brother taught me that.

"So," Stan said again. "Jessie, there's something I want to ask you."

"Wait a minute!" I said, sitting straight up again. "There's something I have to ask you."

I'd been so out of it until that moment, I'd totally forgotten about Rene and the Snuggle Bunny Sock

Hop. By now, I was sure she'd asked Stan to go out with her. I was equally sure that he'd agreed to be her date. In fact, now that my mind was functioning properly, I was sure that the fact that Rene had asked him out was the real explanation behind Stan's phone call. He wanted to know all about her, pump me for information.

"So," I murmured, making my voice all inviting and seductive. Mr. Barnes, my drama teacher, really would have been proud. I was going to make it as hard for Stan to refuse to give me the information I wanted as it was for me not to laugh at his jokes. "Got a Valentine for the Snuggle Bunny Sock Hop?"

"As a matter of fact, I don't. No."

I could feel my whole world exploding in that instant. My body started tingling all over. The hand clutching the telephone receiver went completely numb. I couldn't speak. Couldn't breathe. Only one thought circled madly through my brain.

This time, I had broken my own world's record for blowing it.

I'd sounded exactly like I was about to ask Stan Morris to the Valentine's Dance.

Frantically, my mind raced in a thousand different directions. All of a sudden, I felt a close personal affinity for a rat in a maze. But no matter how hard I thought, my thought always ended up at the same dead end.

With a lead-in like that, there was only one way out of my predicament. Even though it meant a catastrophe of truly epic proportions.

"So," I said, my voice squeaking just a little. "Do you, maybe, want to go to with me?"

There was a pause of a fraction of an instant.

"Well, sure," Stan said, sounding slightly puzzled. "If you want to. I mean, I guess so, Jessie."

It was hardly the most excitement I'd ever generated with an invitation, but I was too freaked out to care.

"Okay," I said my head swimming with despair or relief, I couldn't tell which. "I, um, guess I'll just see you tomorrow, then."

"Okay," he echoed, his voice sounding just as funny as mine did. "Tomorrow sounds good. Good night, Jessie."

"'Night Stanley. Hey, wait a minute," I said, before he could put down the receiver. "What was it you wanted to ask me?"

"What?" Stan said. "Oh, yeah. Well, I guess it doesn't matter. I'll see you tomorrow, okay?"

"Okay," I said. "Bye, Stan."

I heard the soft click of the receiver as he set it back in place. I hung up my phone and stared at the walls of my bedroom. I'm not sure how long it took me to get up the courage to perform the next step. I picked up the receiver and hit the auto-dial button.

"Rene?" I said, when she answered. "There's something I've got to tell you . . ."

"I still don't understand it," Rene said to me at break the next morning. "I don't understand how you could do a thing like this, Jessie."

I took a big slurp of soda and swallowed an ice cube. It made this big lump in my throat.

"I've been telling you and telling you, Rene. I didn't mean for it to happen. It just did. Besides, it's not like I'm the only one to blame. None of this would have happened if you'd asked Stan out the way you said you would."

Rene tossed her head and sent her blonde hair flying. She always does that when she's seriously pissed off.

"Well, excuse me for not organizing my love life to suit you," she snapped back. "And you can just stop trying to put the blame on me. It's not my fault the student council meeting ran longer than Stan expected. And you're always shooting your mouth off without thinking. I told you it would get you into trouble one day."

"I think," I protested, starting to get a little angry in my turn. I'd been apologizing ever since the night before and I was getting a little tired of it. And it really *wasn't* fair to put all the blame on me.

"Oh, sure you do," Rene said, her tone biting. "Well, you want to know what I *think?* I *think* you asked Stan Morris out on purpose. I *think* you deliberately sabotaged me. You couldn't stand to see me happy when you'd blown things, could you? It'd serve you right if I asked John Mulholland to the dance."

"You wouldn't," I said, feeling like I'd taken a punch straight to the stomach. "You wouldn't dare."

"Just you wait and see what I'd dare, Little Miss Boyfriend Stealer."

"He isn't your boyfriend," I all but shouted. "You never got up the guts to ask him to go out with you."

"You never asked John out," Rene shouted back. "So I *think* that means I can ask him."

"You ask John out and I'll never forgive you," I said.

"It doesn't make a difference," she answered. "Because I'm already not forgiving you." She got up from the table and shouldered her backpack. "As of this moment, our friendship is officially over." With those words, she flounced away.

I was left all alone, crushing my soda cup, and wondering how, in the space of twenty-four hours, my entire life had crumbled in on me.

The weeks before the Snuggle Bunny Sock Hop passed slowly. I tried, but I just couldn't get too excited about Valentine's Day. Every time I thought about it, all I could do was to think about how badly I'd blown it. Every time I pictured the dance, all I saw was John Mulholland with his arms around Rene.

She'd asked him to go with her, of course. I don't know how she got the nerve up. But, somehow, she had. Not only that, it seemed like everywhere I looked, I saw the two of them together, laughing and talking. They always looked incredibly happy.

Of course, there were one or two times when I caught John looking over at me. He looked like he had that afternoon I'd dashed madly out of Besto Espresso, kind of puzzled and a little sad. But I told myself it couldn't possibly mean anything. Or if it did, it couldn't mean the things I wanted it to.

As for Stan and me, we were hardly talking. All of a sudden, he was really uncomfortable with me. I tried to tell myself it was just because he was worried about something having to do with the student council. But in my heart I knew it had to do with me.

He didn't want to go to the dance with me, not really. Not anymore than I wanted to go with him. But we were stuck. And all because I'd opened my big mouth. I was so miserable, I was tempted to just sit him down and confess everything to him.

But every single time I came close, I stopped myself. My mouth had gotten us all into this mess. If I said any more, I'd only make things worse. I'd lose Stan, and then I wouldn't have any friends left. So I kept silent, hoping if I didn't say anything else that everything would work out all right in the end.

There was really only one thing I was sure about during those awful weeks. And strangely enough, it had to do with Rene.

She was wrong about Stan and me, that I'd asked him out on purpose, I mean. But, when she'd said our friendship was over, she'd been right on the money. If she really believed I'd deliberately sabotage her, she'd probably never been my friend to begin with.

The trouble was, even though I was hurt and angry, I really missed her.

Under ordinary circumstances, we'd have been getting together every possible spare minute on the days before a big dance. Talking things over and making plans. We might even have suggested to the guys that we go out for dinner beforehand.

That was absolutely out of the question now, of course. It was bad enough to have to watch John and Rene together at school. There was no way I was going to double date with them.

I even had to go shopping for a dress all by myself. For the first time in years that I could remember, I went all alone.

The dress I ended up with was really pretty, though. The saleslady told me it was practically one of a kind. It was made of ivory-colored satin, and it had these tiny pink and red roses all over it. When I put it on, I felt good for the first time in weeks.

I look like somebody's Valentine, I thought as I

stared at myself in the mirror. That's when it occurred to me I was. I just wasn't the Valentine of the guy I wanted.

"Oh, it looks just fabulous," the saleslady cooed, as she turned me this way and that in the mirror. "That retro look is really good on you. A little pair of chunk-heeled red sandals—" she broke off, studying me for a minute.

"And maybe some silk flowers tucked into your hair. You might as well go for the whole look," she said, when she saw my slightly startled expression. "What's the sense in doing it halfway? And we only got in one more like it, so you don't have to worry about anybody else showing up in what you're wearing. You'll be totally unique. I guarantee."

So what can I say? I bought it. And I found the perfect pair of shoes. I bought silk flowers to weave in and out of my hair, and I even splurged on a tube of brand-new lipstick. I took them home and put them away in my closet.

And then I waited for Valentine's Day.

The day of the Snuggle Bunny Sock Hop was truly glorious. There wasn't a single cloud in the entire sky. All over school, couples were holding hands and whispering together. The whole thing just reeked of romance with a capital R.

Naturally this made me feel pretty awful. Stan and I avoided one another all day. I tried not to notice Rene and John sitting together in the lunchroom and in all the classes we shared together. *No doubt about it,* I thought. *This is the world's all-time worst Valentine's Day.*

It was late in the afternoon when the first miracle happened. I was sitting in the outside snack bar catching a few rays. In spite of the sun, the weather was still a little brisk. I didn't have too much competition for a seat. So I was surprised when a shadow fell across my table. I looked up. A dark figure was silhouetted against the sun.

"Hey, Jessie," the figure said.

I swallowed around a sudden lump in my throat. My stomach muscles began to quiver, but I didn't think it was because of the cold. There was only one voice in the universe like that. John Mulholland's.

Somehow I managed to smile at him. "Hey, John." If I kept things simple, maybe I wouldn't screw anything else up. "How's it going?"

John shrugged and eased down onto the bench beside me. "Okay, I guess." I could feel his warmth radiating through his denim jacket. "So," he said. "Happy Valentine's Day."

I have to say this left me absolutely speechless. I couldn't think of a single thing to say. All I could do was sit there, wishing things were different between us.

"Same to you," I finally got out. "Happy Valentine's Day."

John was silent for a moment, his fingers drumming on the bench. For one wild moment, I wondered what would happen if I reached out my hand. If I covered his fingers with mine, would he reject me?

That was when I remembered Rene.

I was sure she didn't really like John. She'd really only asked him out to get back at me. But even so, I had no business expressing an interest in him when she was his date. Particularly not on Valentine's Day. I'd already been wrongfully accused of sabotage once. I couldn't afford to have it happen again.

So I sat beside him, doing nothing.

"Jessie," John finally said. "Would you do me a favor?"

"Of course," I said, the surprise plain in my voice. Then I figured out what he must want. He had a question about Rene. Or maybe he wanted some more pointers about auditioning for the play on Monday.

"Will you save a dance tonight for me?"

I'm here to say, you could have knocked me over with a feather. It's a really good thing I was already sitting down. If I hadn't been, my legs would have given way completely and I'd have collapsed right onto the blacktop.

"Sure," I said, my voice all husky. "I mean, yes, I'd be happy to save a dance for you, John."

There. I'd said it. I'd committed myself and I wouldn't look back. For a few moments, anyway, I could pretend I was having the Valentine's Day I really wanted. I could pretend my Valentine really was John Mulholland.

Stan and I got to the Sock Hop early. I think it's all his time on the student council, but he always feels responsible for things. So naturally he wanted to go and make sure everything was all right. Check with the chaperones and the decorations committee, stuff like that. And I do have to say that the decorations *were* pretty funny.

The walls of the gym were covered with these big white rabbits. The rabbits were wearing these enormous red hearts. About half of them were leaning over, rubbing noses. And there was this big banner over the entrance that said Welcome Snuggle Bunnies.

I still wasn't quite sure about this whole snuggle-bunny thing, myself. But the adult chaperones really seemed to like it, so maybe it was just an age thing.

At long last, Stan finished all his checking. Other couples started to show up and the band launched into its first tune. The band was really good, I do have to say that. It was this great new grunge band called Stud Muffin. We were lucky to get them. They're really in demand.

Stan and I just rocked for a while, until the air in the gym got really hot and I decided it was time to take a breather. That's when I headed off to the bathroom.

Now, the way I see it, a bathroom stop is a must at social events like this. I mean, you've got to check out how your makeup is holding up, right? And the bathroom is the best place to catch up on any late-breaking gossip. I was actually feeling pretty good as I headed off to the bathroom.

Stan and I were speaking to each other again. In fact, we were more comfortable with each other at the dance than we'd been for weeks. Of course, the band had been playing all fast music. They hadn't played any slow dances yet. But even so, I thought we'd manage. And I did have one really important thing to look forward to. The dance I'd promised to save for John.

I hadn't really seen John and Rene that evening, though I did think I'd caught a quick glimpse of the back of John's head. But at the moment I wasn't too worried about it. I was just so relieved that the evening wasn't turning out to be too disastrous.

"So," Helen Walters was saying as I walked into the bathroom. Helen is one of the biggest gossips in the entire school. She also considers herself to be the queen of fashion. "Did you guys see Rene Jackson's dress? It is totally cool."

"Yeah," Susan Parkinson spoke up. "But do you know what else? Jessie Reeves—"

"Hi, you guys. What's going on?" I said.

Conversation in the bathroom ceased abruptly. I found myself the focus of at least six pairs of eyes. Helen made a funny, strangling sort of sound in the back of her throat. She put her lipstick in her purse without even putting the top back on.

"Uh, you look really great, Jessie. We'll see you around." The stampede for the bathroom door reminded me uncomfortably of the stampede for the library door just two weeks earlier. Only this time, I knew there weren't any IEFOs.

All of a sudden, my feeling of well-being vanished. I could swear I heard a chorus of giggles outside the bathroom door. I stood marooned, staring at my dress in the mirror. It looked as wonderful as it always had. I couldn't see a single thing that was wrong.

Then, very slowly, the bathroom door swung open. Another girl walked through the door. I saw blonde hair, swept up on top of her head. A cluster of red roses adorned one side of her hair. On her feet were these great, red chunk-heeled sandals. When she saw me, the other girl stopped dead. Her eyes took in every inch of my attire, then met mine in the mirror.

We were wearing the same dress.

"Hello, Jessie," she said, in a slightly strained voice.

"Hello, Rene."

Now I knew what Susan Parkinson had been talking about. She'd been about to reveal that Rene and I had worn the same dress to the Valentine's dance. It was about the most embarrassing thing that could possibly happen to a person. On top of all the other embarrassing things that had already happened to me, that is.

Rene was still standing behind me, absolutely motionless. I decided I really didn't have all that much to lose. "Nice dress," I said to her reflection.

Just for an instant, Rene hesitated. I could almost see her fighting this fierce battle just by watching the expression on her face. Then she gave up. Her face relaxed and her eyes met mine in the mirror.

"It *is* a nice dress, isn't it?" she said. "I guess great minds really do think alike."

"Either that, or you're a copycat."

That's when it happened. That's when she laughed. The next thing I knew, we had our arms around each other. Then we were laughing and crying and talking all at once.

"I didn't do it on purpose," I gasped out, as soon as I'd recovered enough air to speak. "The saleslady guaranteed me I'd be one-of-a-kind."

"She told me the same thing," Rene said. "I think we should go in together and ask for our money back."

Our laughter subsided and we stood staring at one another. "I'm really sorry I argued with you," I said. I felt it was important for me to say this first, and I wanted to do it before I lost my nerve. "Rene, I've really missed you."

"I've missed you, too," she said. "If nothing else, shopping just isn't the same without you." That made us laugh again. "Seriously, Jess," Rene said, when our giggle fit was over. "I really have missed you. And I'm sorry about all those awful things I said. I didn't mean any of them."

"I know," I said, getting a little teary-eyed again. "I'm sorry, too. But I do have one question."

"What's that?"

"Now what are we going to do?"

Rene was silent for a moment, thinking things over. "I have an idea," she said. "But it's up to you."

"Let's hear it," I answered. So she whispered it to me. I had to admit it was pretty great, though also very risky. But at that point, there really wasn't much else to lose. We left the bathroom together, arms around each other, and set off to put Mission Snuggle Bunny Sock Hop into operation.

In phase one of Mission SBSH, I found Stan over by the punch table, checking on the refreshments. So I had a glass of punch and hung out with him, while I worked up my nerve.

I thought Rene's plan was great. But if the guys didn't go along with it, instead of living happily ever after, both Rene and I would crash and burn.

Stan and I polished off our punch just as the band was getting back from a break. Things would start rocking again any minute. It was time to make my move. My eyes scanned the room for Rene, but I couldn't see her.

"Stan," I said, as we set down our glasses and made our way back onto the dance floor. "We're friends, aren't we?"

Stan look down at me, surprised. "Well, of course we are, Jessie," he said.

"I know this hasn't been the best date in the world, Stan," my words tumbling over one another.

"I'll make it up to you, I promise. But would you do something for me first? As my friend, I mean."

Stan's face looked puzzled, but he spoke without hesitation. "Anything, Jessie," he said. After all the Valentine torture I'd put him through, I was pretty impressed by that answer. I threw my arms around him and gave him a big hug.

"You're the best, Stanley," I whispered.

His chuckle tickled my eardrum. "Of course I am. So, what is this mysterious task I have to perform? Wait a minute. It better not have anything to do with thumbscrews."

This time it was my turn to laugh. "No, Stan," I said. "No thumbscrews. I want you to find Rene Jackson. And then I want you to ask her for the next slow dance."

Well, that went all right, I thought as I watched Stan set off across the dance floor. I wondered if he'd known the way his face had gone all soft and goofy at just the mention of Rene's name. No doubt about it, they were meant to be together.

The band launched into this slow, dreamy number. Which is not all that easy for a grunge band, now that I think about it. But anyway, I was standing there, feeling really happy about Rene and Stan. Once they had the chance to be together, everything was going to work out. When they looked back on this evening, years later, they'd hardly remember that I'd screwed anything up

I did feel a little self-conscious, of course. I mean, I had just sent my date off to dance with another girl. And although I hoped John would come to look for me, I had no guarantee he would. He'd asked me to save a dance for him, but he might not want it to be a slow dance. That made a pretty big romantic statement. So I decided to head back to the refreshment table, where I could try to look inconspicuous.

I'd just turned my back on the dance floor when the second Valentine miracle happened.

"Ms. Reeves?" a voice behind me murmured. My pulse accelerated. I turned around.

"Yes, Mr. Mulholland?" I said, my voice no more than a whisper.

"I believe this is our dance."

To this day, I don't know what happened next. I don't know how we made it to the dance floor. The only thing I do know is that one moment, I was standing by the refreshment table. And the next moment, I was in John's arms.

John's arms felt good around me. Strong and warm and tight. I rested my head against his shoulder, and felt his fingers run up the nape of my neck and into my hair.

"Jessie," he whispered. "I know you're with Stan so I probably shouldn't say this, but holding you just feels so right."

I lifted my head to look at him. Arms locked around each other, we swayed to the rhythm of the dance.

"It feels right to me, too," I said. "And I'm not with Stan, not really. The person I wanted to ask to the dance is you."

"They why—"

"I panicked," I said, before he could finish his question. "When I mentioned the dance when we were having sodas, you got this really weird expression on your face. So I just assumed—"

John interrupted me swiftly. "My mother has this theory about the word *assume.* She says it makes an ass out of *u* and *me.*"

I stared up at him for just a moment. Then I laughed. It was so hokey, yet so right. I certainly had made an ass out of almost everybody, most of all myself.

"I think I like your mother."

"I think my mother likes you, too." John paused for a moment, his eyes intent on my face. "Jessie," he whispered.

Then he did the thing I'd been wanting him to do ever since that moment two weeks ago when I'd first fallen in love with him. He lowered his head and kissed me.

It was wonderful, that kiss. It promised all sorts of things. It promised romance and it promised friendship. It promised love. But most of all, it promised the future, a future as far as the heart could see.

"I don't believe it," a voice next to us said. "Will you look at that?"

John and I jerked apart, instantly self-conscious. It was great that we'd worked things out between us, but maybe we shouldn't have been so public about it. I mean, we had come to the dance with other people. If they saw us, what would Stan and Rene think?

Then I noticed this couple standing a few feet away from us. They were totally wrapped up in each other's arms. The guy was kissing the girl as if she was the last girl on earth. And she was kissing him the same way back. She moved her head, and a spray of red silk roses tumbled out of her hair.

"I thought she came with that other guy," the voice said.

"It's hard to tell isn't it?" his date answered. "I mean, those girls are wearing the same dress."

I wrapped my arms around John, my heart singing with laughter. "Well," I said. "At least we don't need to worry about Stan and Rene."

And so that's how it happened. That's how the most embarrassing situation of my entire life led up to the world's most happy ending.

I even learned a lesson out of all of it. More than one lesson, if you can believe that. I learned I should never make assumptions about what somebody else is feeling. And that, even if it's hard or embarrassing, I should just come right out and say what's on my mind.

What's the other important thing I got out of all this? That I should never, ever, go shopping for a special occasion without Rene. Oh yes, and never carry loose tampons in your purse. Always put them into one of those special little carrying cases. Though, now that I think about it, if I'd followed that lesson, I might never have had such a wonderful Valentine's Day.

Most of the events in this story really did happen to me, believe it or not.

I really did invite the guy one of my best friends was totally in love with to a girl-ask-boy dance. It happened to me pretty much the way it does to Jessie. It started out as a perfectly innocent conversation, and, before I knew what had happened, I heard my voice asking if he had a date to the dance. I was so sure he'd say yes, it never occurred to me there could be any other answer.

When he said no, I wished that I were dead.

It was a feeling I came to know well over the next few weeks as my friend's horrified and disappointed face seemed to follow me wherever I went. But, also like Jessie, my story had a happy ending. Everything got all sorted out in the end. Actually, Jessie's story has a better ending than mine did. The guy in my real-life story wasn't in love with me *or* my friend!

And what about those IEFOs, you ask? Were they a part of my true story? A writer can't reveal all her secrets. So I think I'll let you come up with your own answer to that.

* * *

CAMERON DOKEY lives in Seattle, Washington, where it always rains on Valentine's Day. This gives her the perfect excuse to stay indoors and eat too much chocolate. And sometimes, when her fingers aren't too sticky, she writes a few books. Twelve, in fact. But who's counting?

Wrong Romeo

Sharon Dennis Wyeth

I knew that something was wrong the minute I opened the door and everybody got quiet. But there was no way I could have known that it was about Romeo.

I was going to Mr. Alden's class. It was after school. Mr. Alden is my government teacher, but really young and cool. And I'm not the only one who thinks so. Anyone who counts in the student body at Robeson High is in agreement that Mr. John Alden is the cutest and most progressive teacher we've ever had. A lot of the teachers think so, too, at least the younger ones. That's why after school and during free periods, they hang out in his room.

Myself, I wasn't going to hang out with John. My mother has made it perfectly clear that having a social thing with teachers is off-limits. (She'd die if she knew he let us call him by his first name!) He'd asked me to drop by his room after my Shakespeare rehearsal, because he was helping me to figure out colleges.

Outside, in the hall, I could hear them talking. Ms. Molina even raised her voice. I think she said something like:

"That's outrageous! Has anyone told her?"

Then I walked in and they all shut up.

"Can I help you, Cheri?" Mr. Alden asked.

"You were supposed to talk with me about colleges," I reminded him, shifting the fifty-pound knapsack of books I always seemed to be carrying.

"Ah . . ." his face relaxed some. Then his eyes shifted to the other teachers. Ms. Molina, our new, young biology teacher, has great legs and doesn't mind showing them off. Her skirts are so short, some of the students are taking bets as to how long it will be before the principal, Mr. McGee, will send her to detention for breaking the dress code. I'm sure it will be a first for a teacher. Anyway, she was there in Mr. Alden's room, chewing gum and looking very intense. Mr. Beaty, our red-haired, green-eyed hunk of a gym teacher, was there, too. Obviously they'd been talking about something not meant for youthful ears. Maybe a couple of the teachers were having some kind of affair.

"What's outrageous?" I ventured with a mischievous look in my eye.

"You heard us?" asked Mr. Alden.

"A little bit," I said, hoping they'd let me in on their secret. After all, I was seventeen years old. It's not as if I hadn't heard of affairs.

Mr. Alden cleared his throat and looked at the others.

"Maybe you should let the drama coach handle this," said Ms. Molina.

The three of them stared at me. I suddenly got nervous. "Handle what?" I blurted out.

"I'll take care of this," Mr. Alden said to the other two.

Ms. Molina touched me on her way to the door. "Hang in, sweetie," she said.

"For what it's worth, Cheri," Mr. Beaty chimed in, "I think you're the best all-around student that Robeson has ever had. This shouldn't be happening."

"What the heck is going on?" I demanded as Mr.

Beaty and Ms. Molina disappeared through the door. "Did I do something wrong?"

"Certainly not," said Mr. Alden. He motioned to a chair. "Sit down. And for goodness sake, take that knapsack off. For all the books we hand out around here, the school should have a resident chiropractor."

I let my knapsack slip off my shoulders. It banged into a chair. I ran a hand through my hair. I was sweating. "So, what is it?" I asked.

John perched on one of the desks. "How's *Romeo and Juliet* coming?"

"Great, so far," I exclaimed. I was nuts about drama and totally in love with Shakespeare. "Today was just the second rehearsal. I still have to pinch myself that I got the lead."

John gave me a soulful smile. He has tiny little brown eyes. Until a couple of years ago, there were very few black teachers at Robeson. Which was kind of weird, since Robeson has an awful lot of black students. Now there are about ten blacks on the faculty and John Alden is one of them.

"How's your Romeo?" John asked me.

I thought about the guy playing opposite me—Bruce Bertrand—tall with curly blond hair and wide, blue eyes. His family has a house on Connecticut Avenue. The kind of boy you'd associate with a private school, not with public. Lots of girls think he's good looking. But I'm not attracted. Bruce was in my class in tenth grade and I knew he wasn't smart. In order for me to be attracted to a guy, he has to be not only good looking but intellectual. Besides that, Bruce Bertrand is white. I've never been attracted to a white boy.

"So how is he?" John asked again.

"Bruce is okay," I said. "I guess he might be sick, though. He wasn't at rehearsal today."

"He's dropped out," said Mr. Alden.

"Dropped out? Why would he do a thing like that? He's Romeo. Does he have a conflict?"

"His mother does," said Mr. Alden. "She doesn't want him in the play. Because you're black."

I had an immediate reaction. I felt like someone had punched me. My breath got shallow. And for a minute I thought I might throw up.

Mr. Alden sighed. "Ridiculous, isn't it?"

Tears sprang to my eyes. "This is *Romeo and Juliet!* What does race have to do with it? I mean, this is the dawn of the twenty-first century. It isn't the Middle Ages!"

"Sadly, some people haven't made much progress since the Middle Ages," said Mr. Alden.

"It's a play, for gosh sakes," I fumed. "It's not as if Bruce and I are dating."

Mr. Alden's brow furrowed. "Would there be something wrong with that?"

"Of course not," I snapped. "All I mean is that his mother is being utterly backward and stupid."

"For what it's worth," said Mr. Alden. "I agree."

"I should hope so," I said.

He gave me a meaningful glance. "I haven't talked to anyone else, but Ms. Molina and Mr. Beaty feel the same way. We've got enlightened people teaching here at Robeson, black *and* white."

I shrugged. "So what am I supposed to do? I can't change my race to please Bruce's mother."

The teacher put a hand on my shoulder. "This isn't your problem, Cheri. It's Bruce's loss. You'll still be in the play."

"With no Romeo?" I said bitterly.

"I'm sure the drama coach will find another one."

"Right," I said. "And just when was Ms. Southhall planning to tell me about this?"

Mr. Alden shook his head. "Maybe she wasn't going to tell you. Maybe she was afraid it would hurt your feelings."

"How did she expect to keep it from me?" I demanded. "Half the faculty is already gossiping behind my back. When the kids get hold of this . . ." Tears flooded my eyes.

"You have nothing to hide," Mr. Alden said. I jerked away and grabbed my knapsack.

"Please don't go like this," he called after me.

But I was out of there.

February is a cruel month. Covered with half mounds of sooty snow, the sidewalks long to be washed clean. And the bare branches of flowering trees ache for spring. Of course, the fact that it's Black History month does something to liven things up—there's always a special assembly in school and something of interest going on down at the Smithsonian Museum. But after a while, African dancers and stories about Harriet Tubman seem kind of remote. I mean, what's the point of having a Black History month, when somebody's mother thinks you're an untouchable, just because your skin is brown?

After snatching my parka out of my locker, I'd run outside to the bus stop. My face was still streaked from crying. As usual, it was coming on dusk as I was starting for home. My mother told people that I might as well sleep at school, I loved it so much.

I peered up the street. The wind was bitter. The

bus wasn't coming. I'd forgotten my gloves and hadn't bothered to zip up my parka. Slamming my knapsack onto the ground, I fumbled to zip myself up. But my fingers were already numb and the zipper got caught.

"Shh—ugar!" I screamed in frustration.

A gentle voice startled me. "Is something wrong?"

I turned around. He was standing so close. I hadn't even known he was there. I stared into his hazel eyes. He had curly dark hair. He was white.

"I'm fine," I snapped.

The frown on my face didn't faze him. He moved around in front of me. "Let me try," he said, bending down to look at the zipper. He gave it a tug and freed the flap of caught fabric. Before I knew what was happening, he'd zipped me up.

He smiled and took a few steps backward. "Feel better?"

"Not really," I muttered, "but thanks anyway."

He took a breath and plowed ahead. "I'm Doug McKinley. You're Cheri Smith, aren't you? I saw you at the Shakespeare auditions."

I turned away. At the moment the mention of Shakespeare made me sick. "What about it?"

"I thought you were beautiful."

I turned back around, ready to scowl. But I couldn't. He looked so sincere. "What do you mean by that?"

He hunched his shoulders. "I mean it as a compliment."

"Thank you. I didn't mean to snap on you. I've had a rough day." I let out a breath.

"Sure," he said. "No problem."

The bus came, but he didn't get on.

"Which one do you catch?" I couldn't help asking.

He looked at me and smiled. "I walk."

As I took my seat on the bus, I watched him. His hands were in his pockets. He was very tall. I tried to recall seeing him at the auditions, but I couldn't. But then it came to me that I'd seen him at a basketball game, warming the bench. The bus speeded up. He turned and waved. I didn't look away.

"Things will never change," Mom said. She wiped down the table and wrung out the sponge. "We can legislate laws, but we can't legislate attitudes. Washington, D.C. has always been two cities, a white one and a black one—and never the twain shall meet."

"Mr. Alden says it's Bruce's loss," I told her. My stomach knotted. My mother has a real streak of the righteous. The last thing I wanted was for her to get so riled that she went up to the school.

"Maybe I should just drop out of the darned thing," I said, trying to sound nonchalant. "I've got lots of stuff to attend to. I mean, Shakespeare is archaic."

"You'll do no such thing," she said, wiping down the stove like there was no tomorrow. She turned and put her arm up to her brow. "You auditioned for that part. You will not give up your right to be in the play on account of some addle-brained white woman, trying to protect her precious baby boy."

I laughed. The thought of Bruce as someone's precious baby boy was kind of comical. "He's six-foot-four," I said. "He ain't nobody's baby."

"Well, you're mine," Mom said. She wiped her hands and came over and hugged me. My mom is full of dichotomies. A pencil-thin, gorgeous career woman, her hugs are as warm and full as a fat grandmother's. I sniffed her neck.

"Can I go put on some of your Chanel Number Five?"

"Okay," she said, "but just a touch. I'm almost out of it."

I gave her a kiss and jumped up. "Thanks, Ma."

"Just a minute, Cheri . . ." She reached out to touch my arm, but I slipped away. "About the play—there will be no more talk about dropping out. You go into that rehearsal and hold your head up. As for that Southhall woman, the drama coach—"

"Don't, Mom," I said firmly.

"She handled this thing all wrong. The first person she should have informed about this situation is you. The fact that you heard it through the grapevine—"

"I can handle it," I argued. I gave her a pleading look. "Leave it alone."

Mom let out a sigh. "Can't say that I didn't raise myself an independent. Now, go on upstairs and finish your homework. I'll look over that application to Howard."

"The one to Smith is down there too," I yelled from the stair case. "Don't change anything. They're just the way I want them."

"Relax," she yelled back. "Anybody would think you've got an interfering mother."

What with a Chemistry final and pages to translate in Latin, I was able to push the *Romeo and Juliet* incident to the back of my mind. But when my best friend Debra called, the hurt of what had happened that day bubbled back up inside of me.

"I say it's good riddance," Deb said. She was

trying to bolster me up. "He thinks he's too good to be your Romeo? The fact is, he ain't good enough."

"Thanks," I said mechanically. "But bad-mouthing Bruce isn't going to solve anything. How am I going to face people in school tomorrow? It's so embarrassing."

"You have nothing to be ashamed of," she said hotly. "Bruce's mother is the one who should be ashamed."

"Yeah, but she doesn't go to Robeson. She doesn't have to hear people talking about her."

Deb sighed. "Well, let's look on the bright side. Your new Romeo will probably be Michael." Michael was Mike Harris, a good friend I'd known since first grade.

"Honey, with him playing opposite you, there will definitely be fireworks. I wish I could be in your place."

I giggled. Deb had been carrying the torch for Michael all year, but was scared to let him know. "You know I don't think of Michael that way," I told her. "He's like a brother."

She let out a raunchy growl. "He is *the* brother. The brother of my dreams."

I laughed. "Then what are you waiting for?"

"To lose five more pounds," she said firmly. "Then I'll ask him to the Valentine's Dance. He'll probably say no. But at least I'll look my best when he rejects me."

I shook my head in silence. For years I'd tried to plumb the depths of Deb's self-consciousness. She was on the tubby side, but so what? She had so much else going for her. I was sure that she used her weight as an excuse not to take risks.

"Back to Romeo," she said, breaking the silence.

"I just wish that there was something we could do to get back at Bruce. He insulted you, for gosh sakes."

I suddenly felt so tired and my head was aching. "I have to go. See you tomorrow." I hung up the phone abruptly and turned out the light.

"If love be blind," I whispered, "it best agrees with night." It was one of my favorite lines from the play.

I lay there in the dark.

Why can't the world be blind? I thought. I had never experienced prejudice before. Oh, I knew it was out there. But I hadn't experienced it directly, on my skin. I thought of Bruce's mother. Maybe if she had known me—I'm Cheri Smith, a straight "A" student, number three in my class. I'm president of the Leaders' Club. I was profiled in the newspaper for the volunteer work I've done with retarded children. I sang with my church choir in the Capitol rotunda. Every summer since I was fourteen, I've had a job as a teen model. I'm totally well-rounded—everyone says so. But I'm black. So to Bruce's mother, I'm not acceptable. Maybe if she had known me . . .

I sat up in bed and looked out the dark window. Then I suddenly felt ashamed. There I was, fishing around for something to excuse me from being myself. As if my being number three in the class was something that would make me less black in her eyes. As if being black were something bad. When the fact is that I don't feel that way at all. Being black is just what I am—and as long as I am proud of myself, I'm proud of that.

I lay back down and found my pillow. I began to cry again. The day I'd auditioned for *Romeo and Juliet* a hush came over the auditorium. Something had drawn me in—magic! Magic that had been spoiled.

"Hey." It was the boy from the bus stop. He was in the auditorium. He wore an earring.

"What are you doing here?" I asked. I'd come early for rehearsal. I still hadn't spoken to Mrs. Southhall.

"I got a note from the drama coach," he said, swinging his legs across a chair.

My eyes shifted to the door. "Oh, I thought you were into basketball."

"Forgive me for saying this," he said with a grin. "But did anybody ever tell you that you're beautiful?"

I felt my neck get hot. "Is that your only line?"

He threw his head back and laughed. Some boys with long hair look like girls. His face was sensitive, but he still looked like a boy.

"Sorry," he said, coyly. "I say what's on my mind. The bones in your face are incredible. You should be in the movies."

I rolled my eyes. "Oh, really?"

"And I love your hair," he said, reaching out.

I gave him a stare. "Don't touch me. Don't ever touch me."

He whistled. "Sorry again. I didn't know you were one of those serious sisters."

"I wouldn't presume to touch you," I said. "And yes, I'm very serious. And definitely a sister."

"And I'm just a poor, sorry white punk," he quipped with a sarcastic look in his eye. "But I still like your hair."

He stared at me. "Dare you to laugh."

"What is your problem, man?" I said, laughing in spite of myself. There was something about his stare—I couldn't look away.

He gave me a sweet smile. "Don't mind me. I'm sick."

Mrs. Southhall bustled into the room. In spite of the fact that she was under five feet, she took on the world like a steamroller. "Oh, there you are, Cheri." She stopped dead in her tracks when she saw me. "And you too, Douglas," she murmured, casting a look his way. She came up and took me by the arm. "I have to talk to you."

The rest of the cast was trickling in as Mrs. Southhall led me backstage. I was getting more embarrassed by the minute. *How many people already knew what she was about to tell me?* I wondered. Streaks of afternoon sun made patterns on the floor of the dimly-lit area behind the curtains. Mrs. Southhall stopped and wiped her forehead.

"Hold onto your seat," she said, forcing a smile. "You're getting a new Romeo."

My eyes narrowed. "Is that all you have to tell me?"

She stared at me for an instant, then her face fell. "You know everything, don't you? News travels fast. I struggled with whether or not to bring it out in the open. I'm in a state of shock that this could happen at Robeson. So stupid, really."

"You can't keep something like this quiet," I said flatly. Suddenly I felt claustrophobic. "So, who's Romeo? Mike Harris?" My friend Mike was playing Mercutio. Though he'd been given another part, I figured that Deb was right—he'd be moved up to the lead.

"I'm keeping Mike as Mercutio," Mrs. Southhall said.

I smiled sarcastically. "Well, maybe you'll have to put a sign up: Romeo wanted for jilted Juliet. Must be African-American."

"On the contrary," she said.

I groaned. "You didn't cast another white boy?"

"Doug McKinley. He was my second choice for the role, after Bruce."

"Doug McKinley?" My body jolted with a confusing blend of anger, pleasure, and fear. So, that's why he was sitting out there.

"At the auditions I'd offered him another part," she explained. "But Doug was only interested in Romeo."

"What if Doug's mother has a problem with his Juliet?" I challenged.

"That won't happen," Mrs. Southhall said staunchly. "It can't."

"Why not?" I countered.

She threw her hands up. "I can't control the world—I'm just a high-school drama coach. You are going to be a super Juliet. And Doug is a natural for Romeo. Bruce would have been good, too. But thanks to his mother, he's lost out. End of discussion."

She turned on her heel. "I know this is a hurtful situation for you, and I'm sorry. But we've got a play to put on. And we can't waste another iota of energy on Bruce Bertrand and his mother." She held open the velvet curtain for me and I walked out onstage. The whole cast was assembled. All of their eyes seemed to be on me. Mike was the first to stand up. The others followed and then they all began clapping. Out of the corner of my eye, I saw Doug. Mike waved a fist in the air. "Right on, sweet Juliet!" I didn't know whether to run away or to burst into grateful tears. It was a real show of support.

"Thanks," I muttered, scooting offstage. Quickly finding a seat in the front row, I buried my head in my script. In less than thirty seconds Doug was next to me.

"Hey, beautiful," he said with a wink.

I rolled my eyes. "There goes that line again."

"Just kidding," he said. His smile looked genuine. "I really wanted this part."

I lifted an eyebrow. "What about basketball?"

He shrugged. "It's not much of a conflict. Besides, I'm a better actor than athlete."

"I hope so," I said, alluding to his status as bench warmer.

He put his elbow on the arm of my chair, so that we were touching. "What sign are you?"

"Pisces," I said. "What does that have to do with anything?"

"Just checking," he whispered. "I'm Libra. Air and water go together. That's good chemistry."

I chuckled. "Are you some sort of scientist?"

"No, but you are. My sources tell me you're hot in the lab."

His eyes and tone were flirtatious. I flirted back. "Have you been spying on me?"

"Since the beginning of the year. I'm surprised that you haven't noticed me."

"Well, I haven't," I said.

Mrs. Southhall's voice rang out shrilly. "Keep it down! Can't you see that we're blocking a scene up here?!"

"Sorry," I said.

Doug reached over and ran his finger down the page of my script. "What's your favorite scene?" he asked, in a voice I could barely hear. I felt his breath on my ear.

I turned the page and pointed. I muttered through clenched teeth. "The sappiest part of the play. I must be a sap."

He closed his eyes and whispered. "The balcony scene. I'm a sap, too. Or maybe I just believe in love at first sight, like Romeo did."

"Okay, Romeo and Juliet!" Mrs. Southhall's voice rang out again. "Up on stage. I'm ready for you."

We stood up. Doug got out his script. A strong current was flowing between us.

Just like that.

He reached for me. "Can I try something?"

We were a week into rehearsal. I had come to admire Doug onstage. He had an intuitive way of delivering his lines—Shakespeare's old-fashioned language made perfect sense when he was talking. When he spoke to me he looked right into my eyes, and his voice and face were full of feeling. I was so enamored of the play that I worked overtime memorizing my lines and the blocking that Mrs. Southhall gave to me. But Doug was never a beat behind. In fact he worked ahead in the play, bringing in fresh ideas for stage business. In our excitement we spurred each other on.

"I want to try something different," he called out from the stage. Mrs. Southhall was in the audience. We were going over the scene where Romeo and Juliet first meet at a party.

"We've blocked that," said Mrs. Southhall.

"It feels stiff to me," said Doug. "I'd like to spice it up. Can we experiment?"

"If it's all right with Cheri," said Mrs. Southhall.

He looked at me. "All right?"

I nodded. I admired the way Doug worked our scenes over and over again to make them better. He was a perfectionist, just like me.

"If I profane with my unworthiest hand . . ."

He reached out and touched my hand gently. This was the scene in the play where the two lovers get zapped.

"Good pilgrim, you do wrong your hand too much . . .," I responded.

So far the blocking was what we'd worked out already. But then he took my face in his hands.

"Let lips do what hands do . . ."

And then he kissed me on the lips! I couldn't stop myself from kissing him back.

"What do you think?" Doug asked, twirling away abruptly. Both of us were breathing a bit harder than usual.

"Too hot for Robeson," Mrs. Southhall called back, frowning.

"Oh, come on," said Doug. "This is a passionate moment. Shakespeare wrote the kiss into the play."

"They're in a crowd," argued Mrs. Southhall. "He would never kiss her that way in front of all those people. Kiss her hand, if you have to."

"A kiss on the hand is too formal," I found myself piping up. "Romeo and Juliet are swept away. It's as if no one else exists in that moment. They're in their own little world."

Doug shot me a smile. "Don't forget the scene in *West Side Story* where Maria first meets Tony," he continued to argue. "They dance and touch like crazy. It's totally passionate."

"And *West Side Story* is based on *Romeo and Juliet,*" I added.

Mrs. Southhall put up her hands. "I'm convinced. Just—make it a little kiss, okay?"

I grinned and nodded. Doug turned to me. "Let's do it again."

"Not necessary," Mrs. Southhall said firmly. "We've got to move on."

The rest of the rehearsal, I experienced a heady energy.

"Want a ride?"

I was surprised to see him cruising by my bus stop. Michael happened to be standing there with me.

"Want a ride home?" Doug repeated, leaning out of the window.

The car was an old Volvo. I felt giddy.

"Sure," I said. I turned to Mike. "Come on. Your house is on the way."

Mike lifted an eyebrow. "That's okay, Cheri. Go on with the boy."

I smiled at him distractedly. "Are you sure?"

Mike nodded.

"See you later, then," I called out. "By the way, you're acting up a storm with Mercutio."

I hopped into the car and Doug took off. A buzz went through my body.

"I thought you walked," I said.

"I usually do. Today I borrowed my mother's car." He kept his eyes straight ahead.

The trees whizzed by out the window. "Doing something special?" I asked.

He glanced at me and smiled. "Yes. I'm driving you home."

It was my turn to keep my eyes glued straight ahead as I struggled with a flood of confusing feelings. There was no doubt about it—I liked this guy. Something I definitely hadn't planned on. I told myself it was from all the make-believe we'd been into.

"You've been really nice to me," I said, venturing to break the silence.

He snorted. "You say it like you're shocked."

I saw my reflection in the car window. "I had my doubts at first about your playing Romeo. After what happened with the first one."

"My name is Doug," he said. "It isn't Bruce."

The painful memory made me sarcastic. "So, your parents could tolerate me, huh?"

"We never even discussed it," he said.

"You mean that Mrs. Southhall didn't warn them that your Juliet is a black girl?"

"Did she call your parents to say I was white?" he countered.

We pulled up in front of my house. Doug stopped the car and turned off the ignition. The discussion had gone in a direction that made me feel raw.

He touched my arm. "Race isn't an issue. Not between us."

"It's a big issue in the rest of the world," I reminded him.

His hand was still there. "It doesn't have to be in our world," he said. "We create our own reality."

My heart was pounding. I felt for the door handle.

"I like you a lot," he said.

"And I like you, too," I said lightly. We stared.

"I have to go," I said, breaking the gaze.

"But I have something to say. . . ." His face was suddenly urgent and melodramatic.

"Yes?"

He sucked in a deep breath. "Will you . . . be my Valentine?"

"What?!" I shrieked with laughter.

"Gotcha!" he said. "You're so easy to psyche."

"You're such a weird nerd!" I jumped out of the car. He got out, too, and came around to the sidewalk.

He looked up at my house. "You live here with your mom and dad, huh? Nice."

"Thanks," I said. "My mom and I love it. My dad died when I was twelve."

"Sorry," he said.

We stood next to the car. "That's my room up there," I said, pointing, "the one next to the trellis."

He chuckled. "Don't be surprised if I climb up there one night and knock at your window."

I gave him a skeptical look. "Don't tell me—you're a method actor."

He laughed and found my hand.

"I have it really bad for you, Cheri," he said. "I think you know that."

I caught my breath. "There goes that line."

He held my hand tighter. I turned toward him.

"It's not a line," he said. "I'm serious." He cracked a smile. "I want you to be my Valentine."

We leaned closer toward one another. I'd already tasted his kiss in rehearsal, but then I'd been pretending to be somebody else. Now I wanted to kiss him again, as myself. We slipped our arms around one another and he planted a deep one on me. I broke away, totally zonked by the force of our attraction.

"I could get used to this," he said with a catch in his throat.

"Me, too."

I ran toward the house. "We'd better watch out," I called out playfully. "We're confusing fantasy with reality."

"I'm full of fantasies all right," he called back, laughing.

That night I hardly knew what to do with myself. I felt a combination of restless and exhausted. So I got into bed at 9:30, turned on some soft rock, and clung to my teddy bear. I couldn't get Doug off my mind. Strange and unexpected as it was, I had to admit that Cupid had zapped me. I decided to go with the flow. The phone rang. It was Debra.

"So, how are things going?" she asked.

"Great," I said dreamily. "How about you? You and Michael were talking a lot at lunch today. Any developments?"

"I lost a pound," she announced.

"Oh, please." I sat up in bed. "Deb, I'm sure he likes you. Why don't you just come out and ask him to the dance?"

"Why don't you ask him for me?" she said. "We'll go as a threesome."

"No, thanks," I said. "I think I'd better keep myself on hold."

She giggled. "Someone on the horizon I don't know about?"

I sighed and hugged my knees. "Yeah. Romeo. He's so sweet."

There was silence on the other end of the phone.

"You've got to be kidding. That white boy?"

"He's not a white boy," I said. "He's Doug."

"Doug is white," she said. "And you sound crazy."

"Okay, he's white," I stammered. "So what? He's Romeo. And I kind of like him. He definitely likes me. He told me so."

"I can't believe how dumb you are," she said.

"Thanks a lot."

"Well, somebody has to tell you. Being in a play with him is one thing, but dating is another. His family may be just like Bruce's—they live in the same neighborhood."

"Doug is not Bruce," I said firmly. "Doug has values."

Debra let out a long sigh. "Okay. But don't say that I didn't warn you."

"Relax," I said, slipping back down into bed. "This thing with Doug and me is just a fantasy. It won't last beyond the play. It's nothing serious."

I hung up and turned on the light. Now I definitely couldn't sleep. Though I'd pretended not to buy into her thinking, Deb's comments had really disturbed me. Maybe in Doug's reality race didn't matter, but in hers it did. It mattered in mine, too, of course. Race was something you couldn't get away from in America. It was a national obsession, in every newspaper. In very important ways, identification with a racial group shaped all of our lives. Doug's statement about creating his own reality was so naive. In the midst of my pondering, Mom knocked at the door and walked in.

"You're turning in early," she said. She picked up my shirt off the floor and laid it on the chair. "I got a weird call just now from Mrs. Allbright next door."

"I was talking on my phone, too," I said. "To Debra."

"Mrs. Allbright can be such a busybody," Mom complained. She sat on the side of the bed. "Wanted to know who your boyfriend was."

My face got hot. "I don't have a boyfriend."

Mom laughed softly. "That's what I said. But she insisted that you were necking in a car with a white boy."

I bolted up. "I was not necking in a car! I was talking in a car!" I protested, defending myself with a half-truth.

"Oh, so you were in a car?"

"I got a ride home with my Romeo," I said hotly. "And, yes, as you know, he's white. I can't help that. Mrs. Southhall is the one who cast him."

"You don't have to defend yourself to me," Mom said, getting up. "I already told Mrs. Allbright to mind her own business."

It must have been midnight before I could fall asleep. I'd done a lot of thinking. Why had I told that half-lie to my mother? She gave me a lot of space in my personal life, and the fact that I was kissing a boy wouldn't have shocked her. The truth was that I was sure that Mom would disapprove of the way I felt about Doug, because he's a white boy. Even though Mom knows some whites from work, she has not one white friend. Maybe she just doesn't trust them. After all, in the small town where she was raised, there had been signs for "colored" and "white" on public bathrooms. Mom remembered all that. She even told me a story of how her family was forced out of a new home they'd bought in a white neighborhood. It was a big house. Her family could afford it. My grandfather was a doctor and my grandmother a teacher. But because they were black, their new neighbors had made it impossible for them. Because they were black, they weren't good enough. So, would my mother approve of Doug? Definitely not. Maybe Doug's reality had a spot in it for me, but there was no place in my world for him. I had to nip this in the bud.

The next day when I saw him in the hallway, I turned the other way and walked fast.

"What's your hurry?" he said catching up to me.

"I've got class."

He touched my arm and I felt electric.

"I was wondering if you could meet me in study hall during sixth period. We could find a corner to run our lines."

I gave him a frozen stare. "Don't you think we spend enough time together?"

"Not enough for me," he said.

I pulled away. "I'm busy sixth period."

"What are you doing for lunch?" he called after me.

"Eating with friends."

He was next to me again. "That's right," he said with a laugh. "You sit at the black table."

That stopped me dead. "Excuse me?"

"No offense," he said, backing off. "You do sit at the black table. I've seen you."

"And I suppose you sit at the white table?" I said sarcastically.

He looked momentarily confused. "No, I just sit. I mean, I guess that was a pretty nuts thing for me to say, come to think of it. You don't sit with them because they're black. You sit with them because they're your friends. That's right, isn't it?"

"Yes," I said tersely. "Those friends have names—Debra and Michael."

He shrugged. "Sure, Mercutio. Maybe Mike and I can run our lines, too."

I swung around and leaned against a locker. "You just don't get it, Doug. There's nothing going on between us. So, stop trying to pretend that there is."

He looked as if he'd been stung. I think there were tears in his eyes.

"Here," he said, stuffing something into my hand. "I was going to give you this on Friday. At the dance. I hadn't asked you yet, but I was so sure that you would say yes."

I looked down. In my hand was a cut-out red valentine.

"Dumb, huh? But what can you expect from a white boy?"

I watched him walk down the hall. I felt like the breath was knocked out of me. I'd tried my hardest to be mean and I'd succeeded. I turned away and tears sprang to my eyes. What had Doug done to deserve such treatment? I felt ashamed.

That afternoon at rehearsal, we hardly looked at each other. There was no connection between us in the scenes. I felt dull and lifeless during my monologues. In the scene where Juliet impatiently waits for nightfall so that she can meet Romeo, the lines suddenly sounded ironic. "If love be blind, it best agrees with night," I said. The words echoed in my brain. "If love be blind . . ."

When I left school, he was nowhere in sight. At home, I locked myself in my room. I sprawled out on the floor and stared at the ceiling. Then I heard a pebble hit my window. I looked out. Doug was on the front lawn.

I ran downstairs.

"I'm sorry about today," I blurted out, running

onto the lawn without my coat. My voice choked. "It's just that—"

"I'm the one who came to apologize," he interrupted. Against the gray sky, his face looked so earnest. "What I said about my being just a 'dumb white guy'—well, that was a low blow on my part. I'm sure that can't be the reason that you don't like me. I've been coming onto you like crazy and I'm sorry. I thought I felt this thing between us."

I touched his arm. "You do. And I feel it, too."

He pulled me close and held me. "Cheri, oh Cheri. I love your name. I could say it over and over."

I put my head on his chest. "Romeo, oh Romeo," I teased, "you've had an overdose of Shakespeare."

"I liked you before the play," he said, running his hand through my hair. "At the audition, I thought you were so incredible. I mean, you're so smart. Not many girls I know are interested in Shakespeare. But that day when you screamed at the bus stop—you looked so wild and dramatic and sexy."

I groaned and hid my face. "I'm sure I looked like a nut. That was when I found out about Bruce dropping out. I was mortified."

He touched my face. "Bruce is a jerk, just like his mother. I'm not."

I touched one of his curls. I ran my finger over his earring. "You're a really nice person, Doug. But you were right. I was judging you today because you're white."

He put his hands in his pockets and looked up. "Don't tell me that your mother wouldn't approve?"

"She might not," I said. I came closer. "To tell the truth, I'm kind of afraid. People might talk."

"Let them."

"I've never been attracted to a white boy," I told him.

"There's always a first time," he joked. "Besides, don't forget love is blind."

Then we kissed by the trellis. Right in my front yard. I didn't care who saw. Not even Mrs. Allbright.

Later that night, I spoke to Mom. "I'm going to the dance on Friday. I've got a date."

"Oh, yeah?" She looked up from the paper.

I smiled. "I'm going with Romeo."

"The one who drove you home that day?" she asked, turning the pages.

"He's white," I said.

"You know that I know that."

I peeked over her shoulder. "Do you mind?"

She looked at me squarely. "I can't lie and say that it doesn't make me a bit nervous. I didn't know a single white person when I was your age. So, I never visualized it for you. But your life is different from mine. And though we're mother and daughter, we're two different people. Besides," she added, peering over her glasses, "I'm not going to judge the boy before I get to know him. Who do you think I am? Mrs. Bertrand?"

"Oh, Mom . . ." I hugged her. "Wait until you meet him," I exclaimed. "He's applied to Yale Drama. He's also applied to UCLA. Law school might interest him later."

"You seem to know a lot about him," she said, standing up.

"We talk a lot in rehearsals," I gushed. "If he decides on Yale and I get into Smith, we'll both be on the East Coast. If I decide to go to Howard, it's still not that far."

Mom smiled and shook her head. "Take things a little at a time. It's just your first date."

Thursday night after school, Debra came over. "What are you wearing?" she asked.

I opened the closet and took out a long, batik skirt. She squealed. "I love that!"

"It was my mother's," I explained. "I've been begging for it." I grinned at myself in the mirror. "I've got some brand-new gold hoops for my ears and I'm going to douse myself with Chanel Number Five."

Debra grinned. "That boy is not going to know what hit him."

I turned to her. "I know you think it's stupid that I'm going with Doug. Thanks for not rubbing it in."

"I can't talk you out of anything," she said, examining her fingernails. "Besides, I want you there to hold my hand tomorrow."

"You're going?"

She nodded. "With Michael. I asked him and he said yes."

I threw my arms around her. "Way to go, girl! I bet he was pleased."

She shrugged shyly. "He seemed to be. He told me that he'd wanted to ask me himself, but he'd been too nervous."

"He's very sensitive," I said. "We shouldn't assume that all boys are tough."

Debra took a long look at herself in the mirror. "Of course, I haven't lost that five pounds."

"Don't worry about that, Deb. You're beautiful."

"So are you," she said. "I've never seen you look happier."

She sat down on the bed and I sat down beside her.

"Where will we all be next year, Cheri?" she said dreamily.

"Who knows?" Doug's valentine was propped up on my dresser. "All we can do is enjoy today. And leave the rest to tomorrow."

We lit a candle.

I'll never forget the night of the dance. Everyone seemed to be smiling. Debra and Michael and lots of the cast from the play were there. When Doug and I walked in, Mr. Alden greeted us. He shook Doug's hand and gave me a kiss on the cheek. "You look positively ravishing, Cheri," he said.

I giggled. "Thanks, John."

As Doug and I walked onto the dance floor, we passed Ms. Molina and Mr. Beaty, almost as engrossed in each other as we were. If anybody had a problem with Doug and me as a couple, we certainly didn't notice. With every molecule of our beings, we were riveted to one another.

"You're a good dancer," he said. The first dance was a slow number.

"So are you," I said easing in closer. We moved in perfect synchronicity.

But then the tempo picked up. He twirled me wildly. Our dancing styles seemed suddenly at odds. I saw Debra and Michael off to one side, giggling at us mischievously.

"Why are you suddenly so wild?" I hissed. He twirled me again, nearly yanking my arm out of its socket.

"You have that effect on me," he said, jokingly. He shook his head, trying to be more outrageous. I giggled and he pulled me in close. "You make me crazy, baby. I'm just cutting loose. But since we're in public, I'll try to act cool for you. . . ."

After the dance, we walked out to the car. It was starting to snow—winter's last desperate attempt. Doug held my hand. My heart did a flip.

"I think I love you," he said.

A shiver ran up my back. "There goes that line."

"When something is true, why not say it?" Doug said quietly. "I know what love is. And I feel it."

Then I let myself melt into his kisses.

I'll always remember how his arms felt—safe and warm. His neck smelled delicious, like strawberry soap.

"I love you, too," I whispered. I looked up. His dark curls were covered with snow.

"We'd better go," he said, brushing my coat off. "You have snow on your eyelashes." He steered me toward the car. "I promised my parents that I'd bring you by for hot chocolate."

My bubble burst with a thud. Since that one brief mention that day in the car, the subject of Doug's parents hadn't come up. I couldn't help wondering what kind of reception they'd give me. "It's snowing," I hedged. "Maybe we should go home. My mother might be worried."

"We can call her from my house," said Doug. "My dad can drive you, if the weather gets too bad." He patted my hand. "I met your mother when I picked you up. Now it's your turn."

Though the neighborhood was somewhat fancier, Doug's house was pretty much like the house that I lived in, with the living room and dining room on either side of a foyer. His mother was sweet and genuine. She looked older than my mother. If his parents were surprised that my skin was brown, their faces didn't register it.

Doug's father made the hot chocolate. He was so careful—measuring the milk and cocoa meticulously, as if making us hot chocolate was the most important thing he'd ever done. Once our drinks were steaming in the cups, he put marshmallows on top. I was hooked. My own dad had loved marshmallows. One of my favorite memories of him was when we were on a family camping trip and he was making s'mores.

"Doug tells me that you're interested in medicine," Doug's father said, carefully handing me a cup. I blew on it.

"My grandfather was a doctor," I said. "It must run in the family."

"Having a career and a family can be hard," warned Doug's mother. "I went back to working in a law firm full time when Doug was thirteen. It wasn't easy breaking back in. And with things here at home to do, I felt like a juggler."

"I know," I said. "My mom has always worked. Anyway, I'm a little young to be thinking about the family part."

"What field is your mother in?" asked Mr. McKinley.

"She's a clinical psychologist," I said. "She has her own office downtown. But she also does a lot of consulting for the courts."

Doug's dad ended up driving me home. Which made it kind of awkward when Doug walked me to the door. By now it was snowing heavily and everything was hushed and blanketed.

"I had the greatest time," he said, kissing me lightly.

"Me, too."

Mom opened the door. She'd been pretty formal with Doug earlier that evening, but now her face looked softer. "Hi, Doug." She smiled. "Thanks for getting her home safely."

He smiled back. "No problem."

"Would you like to come in?" she asked. Mom's face looked so pretty in the lamp light.

"Another time," he said. "My mother's waiting for me and my dad."

Mom waved at Mr. McKinley in his car, and he waved back. Doug looked at me. His eyes were twinkling.

"Bye," he whispered. "Talk to you tomorrow."

Mom and I went in. I went straight to the window to watch Doug's car drive away. Moonlight shone on the driveway.

"How was it?" asked Mom.

"It was the most beautiful Valentine's Day I've ever had," I told my mother.

Three weeks later, we opened the play. Everyone said it was brilliant. Michael was amazing as Mercutio, especially in the sword-fight scenes. Deb was there every performance in the front row, swooning. As for Doug and me, the play took us away on our own magic carpet. Swept up in the beauty of the language and the romantic plot, we became the young lovers created by Shakespeare. In the scene where Romeo and Juliet first meet, I felt the thrill of our first meeting. When our hands touched, I felt fire. In the spot in the play when the young couple gets married, I experienced what it must be like to want to fully commit yourself. And in the tragic ending, when Romeo dies and Juliet follows him, I cried real tears. Of course, deep down we both knew that it was all make-believe. Especially the dying part. As we lay there side by side onstage, pretending to be unconscious, Doug tickled me and I smothered a giggle.

The audience's applause knocked me out. Everyone was so nice. Mom came backstage and so did Doug's parents. But Mrs. Southhall was the first to congratulate us.

"You were perfect," she said. She put a chubby hand on each of our shoulders. Her eyes got teary. "It was so believable."

As if the night couldn't be more perfect, there was still the cast party and afterward. For a brief moment when Doug and I were wolfing down pizza with the cast, I thought of Bruce Bertrand. He must have seen the play—the whole school had. I wondered if he thought that he'd missed something. One thing was for certain, I was glad that Doug had taken his place.

"I love you," he said, kissing my fingertips. We'd found a corner where we could be alone.

I kissed him full on the mouth. "I love you, too."

He made a fake grimace. "What will I do without you next year? My soul is aching."

I leaned my head on his shoulder and smiled. "You're so dramatic," I teased.

The school year sped by. Our romance didn't wane. Before we knew it, graduation day had arrived. My grandparents had come up from the South for the ceremony, and Doug had family there, too. Doug and I hardly saw one another.

Then the year was over.

There were a couple of achingly romantic dates

over the summer. We went to see a revival of *West Side Story*. I was going to Smith in September. He was going to UCLA. August was an endless good-bye.

One night especially sticks in my mind. We'd just seen a breathtaking performance of the Alvin Ailey dance company. Doug looked into my eyes and touched my neck. I took in every inch of his face.

"You've got a freckle on the end of your nose," he teased. "It's so small, I can just make it out."

I laughed. "And right over by your ear, you've got a small zit."

He kissed me. "You're so mean."

"That's why you love me," I said.

He touched my cheek. "I do," he said. "Don't forget that. . . ."

So now it's one year later. And next week is Valentine's Day. Doug and I have kept in touch the best we can. College is a trip—it's so different! So many people to meet, including guys. So much to learn. So many things to do. I'm taking a lot of science courses. I think of myself as pre-med. There are several other black girls in my dorm. We spend a lot of time together. My roommate, Holly, is white, with blond hair and blue eyes. She's smart and has a great sense of humor. We're both excited about our new friendship. Debra and Michael both went to Howard. I really miss them. Of course I know that Deb and I are friends for life.

I saw a casting ad for a play in the student paper and I'm thinking about auditioning. I spend an awful lot of time in the library. Some nights I'm so exhausted I can't remember anything about Washington, except my house and my mother. Caught up in the college scene, some days Doug is a distant memory. But when his letters arrive, my heart starts to race and the feelings we had for each other come flooding back.

I have the valentine he gave me in the drawer of my dresser. I don't think anything could top it. A simple red heart made out of construction paper. He'd cut little stars in the border. He'd written his message in calligraphy. When I read the words, I see his beautiful hazel eyes with all their intensity.

"There never was a greater love," Doug wrote, *"than Romeo's for his sweet Juliet."*

Sharon Dennis Wyeth

Valentine's Day was always a nightmare for me. The anticipation of whether or not I was going to get a valentine was so excruciating! But I do remember the first box of candy I ever received—from my dad! I didn't see him all that much, so it was really special, especially at the age of seven when I didn't think much about boys. Every morsel of candy was scrumptious and the smell in the box remained for months afterward.

When I got older things did heat up somewhat, especially when I began to date a very cute boy. I'll never forget the mystery valentine I received—a string of tiny red tissue hearts, meticulously cut out, with a tiny question mark penned in place of a signature. Assuming that it was from my current boyfriend, I immediately ran out and bought him a baseball cap that I knew he'd had his eye on. When I presented him with my present and complimented him on his paper-cutting ability, he modestly admitted his identity as my mystery valentine But a problem arose when my best friend called me that night and ecstatically reported that she'd gotten a mystery valentine, too, identical to my own! The next day I checked her valentine out; it was precisely like my own, right down to the penned question mark in the corner. It seems that my "boyfriend" had his eye on my best friend! My best friend was appalled and I was kind of angry and a little bit jealous. When my boyfriend told me that he had sent a valentine to my friend because he felt sorry for her, I wasn't convinced. Just like he'd cut that tissue paper, I cut him out of my heart. I figured a loyal girlfriend was better than a two-timer!

SHARON DENNIS WYETH has written for daytime television, as well as the children's program "Reading Rainbow." Her books include *The World of Daughter McGuire, Always My Dad,* and "The American Gold Swimmers" series. The incident described in "Wrong Romeo" is drawn from her own life experience. The walls of her office are plastered with valentines she's received from her husband, daughter, and readers.